Outside

Follow Sarah Ann Juckes
on Twitter and Instagram
@sarahannjuckes
@sajuckes
www.sarahannjuckes.com

Outside

SARAH ANN JUCKES

PENGUIN BOOKS

PENGUIN BOOKS

UK | USA | Canada | Ireland | Australia
India | New Zealand | South Africa

Penguin Books is part of the Penguin Random House group of companies
whose addresses can be found at global.penguinrandomhouse.com.

www.penguin.co.uk
www.puffin.co.uk
www.ladybird.co.uk

First published 2019

001

Text copyright © Sarah Ann Juckes, 2019

The moral right of the author has been asserted

Set in 10.75/15.5 pt Adobe Caslon Pro
Typeset by Jouve (UK), Milton Keynes
Printed and bound in Great Britain by Clays Ltd, Elcograf S.p.A.

A CIP catalogue record for this book is available from the British Library

ISBN: 978–0–241–33075–3

All correspondence to:
Penguin Books
Penguin Random House Children's
80 Strand, London WC2R ORL

To everyone who believed

Once upon a time,
there was a girl who lived in a Tower,
and she was alone.

PART ONE

INSIDE

ONE

Here's the thing about being Inside. Ain't no one believes that they are.

Pretty stupid, as there are clues just about all over. Feed rattling down pipes from somewhere else. That dirty ol' smell on Him when He barges in through the door.

And the door. And Him.

But the Others, they stick their fingers in their ear holes and tell me to quit with my lies. They're as happy as can be Inside these four walls. They eat when it's time to eat. Sleep when it's time to sleep. Read when it's time to read. Far as they see, ain't no need to see no Outside.

Or maybe they're just scared.

Not me, though. I'm gonna get me my proof.

TWO

Tonight's the night before He comes. I'm trying not to think about it, but here it is, sneaking into my head anyway.

The dark don't help none. I reckon the sun bars turned themselves off early tonight and the whole Tower is stuffed full of shadowy thoughts now.

I can hear the Others sleeping all together. I can't see them, but I've been seeing them just about every day of my life, so I got a clear picture of them pasted on my eyeballs. They'll be tangled up in each other – heads tucked under armpits resting on backs. Queenie will be buried with Cow someplace, ass in the air and glowing like a broken moon. Cow will be turned my way, his head out proud in all its hairless glory, his big ol' eyes closed behind droopy eyelids. His nose – the biggest of all of them – will be hooked over Bee's foot, sniffing the day off her.

There'll be space in there for me if I want it, too. I ain't gonna fill it, though.

I ain't got their small heads and pointed ears. I've got yellow hair, like Rapunzel, and a small nose, rounded ears and skinny body, like the Outside People I see in my books. I don't look like the Others. The only things I've got are their long fingers – thin as keys. Not a lot those fingers can do, though, without a lock to pick.

I don't belong to them. They want me to – but I don't.

I know I should be sleeping, tomorrow being the day that it is, but I'm feeling more awake than ever.

I scrape the tips of my fingers along the wall, feeling for the soft part.

Once upon a time, there was a girl who lived in a Tower, and she was alone.

I knock the line out. *KNOCK-knock-knock-KNOCK-knock-knock.*

I wait, not breathing hardly. It's so dark that the blinking red light above the door could be some kind of lighthouse.

You're not alone.

Jack. He's awake. His knocks come quiet and I need to listen real close to hear them.

I let out my breath, moving myself closer to the wall so the coldness eats up the insides of my bones.

Her Tower was guarded by Goblins.

Ele, Goblins again?

Yeah, I knock. *Goblins. They lived with her Inside the Tower and they told her she was lying about there being an Outside, but she weren't. She was telling the truth.*

How do you know?

I rub my thumb over my knuckles, and I tell him again.

The Proof of the Outside – number one: Books.

Books are truth and they all show the Inside and the Outside. Outside is trees and gingerbread houses. Inside is walls.

We got three books. *The Alphabet Book. An Encyclopaedia of British Trees. My First Book of Fairy Stories.*

Books are my windows. They show me everything I need to know to be an Outside Person, from killing Dragons to growing beanstalks. It'd be awful dark Inside without no books.

The Proof of the Outside – number two: The door.

In the books, doors are how you get from Inside to Outside. It's how He goes from Inside to Outside.

It's how I'll go too, I reckon.

But, Ele, why do you want to be Outside if He is Outside?

Stop interrupting.

The Proof of the Outside – number three: Him.

He smells of it – cold and sour, like wall. He brings things from it as proof for me – like the books. He tells me of it sometimes, too, when He's not in a mood. Just little things, like what 'glass' is, and how it gets stuck in your foot if you break it, or how it gets 'mighty hot out there sometimes'.

I gather all these things up like breadcrumbs, showing me the way.

But He does bad things, too. You can't trust Him.

I ain't scared, I knock back.

The Proof of the Outside – number four: Me.

I look at those people in the books and they look just like me – hair long and wild, noses and ears all round, lips puffed up and red as apples. They're all walking paths and climbing trees. Even Rapunzel, locked in her Tower, goes and gets freed eventually.

I don't belong here – not one bit. I got to get back to that Outside or I'll die.

You won't die, Ele.

I might. He's killed before, remember?

Silence.

The Others will protect you.

I let Jack think they do, 'cause it'd hurt him something awful to think that they don't. But no one is supposed to move when He's in. And Zeb – Zeb was stupid for trying. And He went and did *that* to Zeb's head and – and –

I don't want to talk about Zeb, I knock.

I understand.

I'm sorry.

It's OK.

I put my forehead on the wall and I close my eyes until the cold sinks into my skull and numbs it right up. The silence is making me all itchy, so I squeeze my eyes up tight and knock out the last proof real quick.

The Proof of the Outside – number five: Zeb is gone.

It wasn't your fault, Ele.

I don't reply.

Ele?

7

I keep my eyes closed for the longest time. It's so dark that I can't even tell no difference.

What do you look like, Jack?

I poke my finger around my smooth fist-shaped bit of wall, wishing I could poke a hole right through it and see his eye watching me from the other side. The wall was as rough as ol' skin when we started talking – about the time that Zeb went, and everything changed with the Others. I was feeling mighty alone and, just like that, his knocks were there. And I knew – I knew what they were saying to me like it weren't nothing at all. 'Cause Jack and me, we're magic. And that's all there is to it, OK?

I don't know, he knocks back.

I press all of me to the wall and imagine Jack doing the same on the other side. And I'm wishing the wall was warm so I could feel him next to me.

I'm going to go to sleep now. His knocks come out sleepy.

I want to talk more, but I've gone and run out of proofs.

OK.

I don't sleep. I can't.

He's coming.

The red light above the door counts down those seconds, and each flash is like another little heartbeat that's gone and been snuffed out.

THREE

Zeb is in my dreams. It's a memory, I reckon. We're young and we're playing a game, hiding away from something. I'm trying to keep quiet, but giggles are bubbling up in my throat. Zeb's hands are over my mouth, and mine are over his. I can feel his smile between my fingers.

Then we hear footsteps. I can feel his heart in his lips, beating even faster than mine. The footsteps get closer and I shuffle nearer to him, pressing my head into the side of his neck.

He smells like everything. Inside and Outside, all wrapped up in leaves.

The footsteps stop. Zeb's giggling too now. His chin holds me right to him.

'Found you.'

And I turn and look. But I don't see no Others. I don't even see Him. I see a lady. A lady with yellow hair and red lips pulling back a smile.

I wake up with a start.

It's only dark for a moment before the sun bars flick on and blast my open eyes clear out my head. Ain't no time to sit thinking about the strange lady in my dream, or hiding away like the Others are doing, their heads all shoved into each other. I got just about enough time before the feed comes down to do my thing.

I jump up. I can't tell you how good it feels to stand on legs. If you ain't tried it before, I recommend you do. These few moments where I get to act like a real-life Outside Person, rather than an Other, are the greatest in my whole day. Especially on a day like today.

I get running. Running with my legs wide and my arms flapping out like I'm a Dragon who's gonna take off and fly into the sun bars on the ceiling. This was Zeb's thing. He made us get up as soon as those sun bars came on and we wouldn't stop 'til we couldn't stand up no more.

I run faster and faster, until my breath is so loud that I wonder if it'll suck the door right out, and it feels almost like Zeb's here again, running next to me. I smile wide. And, when I'm pretty sure I'm awake, I bend forward on to my hands, my fingers pushed out as wide as they'll go, with my elbows bent. Then I rock forward even more and kick my feet up until I'm standing right on my hands.

The Tower looks mighty different from upside down. The sun bars are on the floor now, locked in their criss-cross cage so we can't smash them. They're humming their light out bright, all three of them. And the floor is my ceiling, with the drain in the middle and the food bowl upside down like me.

I start bending my elbows and try to get the top of my head on the floor. My body is shaking something terrible, but I focus on keeping my feet as straight and still as I can. I manage to go down once all right, and then I push myself back up again. *One.*

I try for two, but my whole body is shaking like mad now and I'm worried that I'm gonna fall on my head again like last time. I screw my eyes up tight, though, and focus on breathing slowly. I start going down and make it so I can feel the floor pricking at the shortest hairs on the top of my head. I squeeze my belly in tight, wrap my feet together and push myself back up again, my arms buckling and nearly throwing me right over. But then! My elbows finally lock out and I roll myself back down on to the floor, breathing like I've been running all night.

Two.

A new record, and I'm right proud. I know Zeb would be too, if he was here. Won't be long until my arms are as thick as a Giant's and can break through walls. Here's hoping.

Ain't no time to get my breath back, so I hop up quick on to my feet again. I jump up, round, down and out. I twirl faster and faster. I kick my legs out behind me and try to touch them with my arms. I don't make it, but I will.

I will I will I will.

Cow makes a noise like he knows it's nearly feeding time, so I drop myself back down and pretend as best I can that I ain't been up to nothing. They get awful sad when they see me acting like an Outside Person – and you don't get much more Outside than running. I might as well be a Prince being chased by an Ogre when I'm doing that.

Two, though. Two! I'm getting stronger, and it won't be long now 'til I get more proofs, just you wait and see.

The walls start clacking and the feed comes down from the pipe sticking out of the wall opposite me, filling the whole Tower with noise. I can hear the Others grunting and kicking at each other for first dibs, but I just stay curled up, trying to get my breath back.

I don't normally eat on days like today.

I watch them from between my knees, stuffing handfuls of the brown balls inside their mouths, crunching down on them like Giants eating bone bread. The feed bowl is standing off the floor using its little legs, but it's still low enough that you got to eat out of it on your hands and knees. It's long enough for all of us to be eating from it at once, if we don't mind hitting elbows.

I don't like the feed much anyway. It smells like armpits and tastes like the bowl itself – what He told me was 'metal'. Same as the tap sticking out of the wall next to the bowl, even though that's brown rather than silver, and not black like the cage over the sun bars on the ceiling and the drain in the middle of the Tower, or grey like the door.

They're all metal too, but different types. I know.

The door is in the corner furthest from mine. You can get there in six long strides. He can stride over in five. You'd probably think it was just another bit of wall with an arm bending from it if it wasn't for Him bounding on through it every seven days.

You got to have a key to use it and He's the only one with one of them. It's as flat and as white as pages, and about as long as a finger. He taps it easy on the box next to the door and the red light above goes green, just like that.

The box don't make the light green for nothing else that looks like pages – just that key. That one is magic.

That's about all that's Inside, apart from the cricks and cracks in the walls and floor that I know like they're part of me. And the books, hiding under the bowl. And the four of us.

It's not much like the Tower in 'Rapunzel'. She has all kinds of things Inside with her, like tables and chairs. Her Tower is high up in the sky, too. I ain't sure if we're up or down in here, but we call it the Tower anyway. Towers are places where people are kept Inside.

At least I got my Others, though. Rapunzel must have been awful lonely in there by herself until that Prince came up her hair.

The Others are sitting round the bowl, licking at the feed they've dropped over themselves. They're doing it fast, mind, as pretty soon the walls start clacking again and the sun bars rain water on us all, freezing our bones up and making us all squeal out.

I like to think of it as rain – like the rain in the books – but it ain't even half as blue as that, and it tastes much worse than the water from the tap. When I get Outside, first thing I'm gonna do is find me some real rain.

The water slows to drips and I wipe my hair out of my face – heavy and flopping down my back. I squeeze it out as best I can, else it gets awful cold.

I'm watching the Others to see what they do, as they know it's getting to that time. They're keeping busy, giving themselves their own clean with their tongues, or taking the books out of the hiding place under the bowl and looking at the pictures. Bee's even giving them a read. I can see her lips moving.

Queenie's watching me. She knows what I'm gonna do.

I shuffle over there like an Other. It's easier with the water still puddling before it gets sucked down the drain. My legs straighten out, my heels grip the floor, and I pull my ass forward. Shuffle, shuffle.

I look at the drain. I can still see the stain Zeb's head made, getting smaller, but still there. Long and red, curling right round the black bars like a Witch's finger, and disappearing down.

I push my eye up close to the drain and wonder if I could make myself so small that I could trickle down there after it. Then I feel her on my back and at my ear.

'Cow says he wants to play. Ain't you gonna come play with us, Ele?'

Queenie. I shake my head.

She grabs my arm, pulling at me to turn round and look at them. At Bee's eyes all excited about getting to play Rapunzel. At Cow jumping up at the thought of a wrestle.

I pull my arm away, staring at Zeb's blood on the floor.

She moves round me to my other ear.

'You'd feel better, you know, if you stopped thinking on that boy and that stupid made-up Outside.'

I keep my hands out flat, even with them twitching to ball up tight. 'I ain't thinking nothing but truth.'

She starts grunting beside me, like my words have bitten her. She moves in close and hisses real slow in the language of the Others, exaggerating all the clicks her mouth makes as she says it.

'Liar.'

I turn quick and arch my back up, but I don't take her by surprise. She's already up on her fingertips, baring those teeth at me and puffing herself out all big. I catch Bee behind her, eyes wide and scared. Cow shakes his head, looking sad.

I close my mouth and back off.

Queenie sits down, right on top of poor Zeb's head stain.

I scowl at her. At all three of them. They say Outside is all lies. And they won't have me thinking of Zeb neither 'cause, to them, as soon as something ain't Inside no more it ain't real. If it was up to them, we'd all still be rolling around like little 'uns, living in our lies.

I ain't scared of no truth. I remember.

Zeb looked like me, 'cept he was a boy. He had the same pale skin, same long fingers, same bones sticking out. When he let me touch him, I used to close my eyes and map our faces out with my fingers, and they were the same, too. Nose, eyes, chin, cheeks. His jaw was a little squarer, like a page with the corner folded over. And his hair was a bit darker than mine and not quite as long, though it sat down below his shoulders easy by the time it happened. When his eyes looked at me, as wide and blue as the sky Outside, and his hand stretched out towards me.

A hand like mine.

I rub the pain building up in my chest. He'll be here soon, the man who took Zeb. Soon as that water dries off the floor, we'll hear Him.

I sit with my back against Jack's wall. It's calling to me, but I can't knock to him in front of the Others. They reckon I'm crazy enough as it is. They wouldn't understand the magic of his knocks.

Instead, I fold myself in real close. I think about that lady's face – the one in my dream. I ain't never seen her before, but her red smile is hanging around my eyes like I've been looking at the sun bars too long.

Maybe she's a Princess, too. Come to life out of the books while I was sleeping.

And I'm thinking on that when I hear the whistling. I'm hoping it's just the ringing in my ears. I've found they're awful prone to doing that on days like today. Seems like every minute is a new whistle. But this one don't do nothing but get louder, and pretty soon the Others are whimpering and shuffling away from that door about as fast as their asses will take them. They pile together in what used to be Zeb's corner – the one next to mine when we're looking at the door.

I sit on my hands and squeeze my eyes up tight.

Whoo-oo-who-oo-oo-ooo.

'Ele,' one of them is saying. 'Ele.'

Don't know which one it is or what they want, but I'm praying they keep their mouth shut, as I'm trying my damnedest to stop the scared coming up inside of me.

We hear the clang from far away and the whistling gets louder. Same ol' whistle.

Whoo-oo-who-oo-oo-ooo.

'Ele.'

Shutupshutupshutup.

I can hear His footsteps now, loud as can be. What are the names of the trees?

OakWillowBirchSycamore–

'Ele!'

MapleAshPine–

And then the footsteps stop and I'm all out of trees, 'cause the light above that door's gone and turned green.

Ain't no one saying my name no more. All heads are to the floor, all bodies about as far away from mine as they can get.

He won't see them anyway. He'll just see me. Just like He never saw Zeb 'til he stood up.

He pushes the door open and I try to slow it down, so I remember to look past Him to what's behind Him, but ain't no seeing that. I forget what breathing feels like and all I see is that grubby face of His, those cheeks like someone has slapped them. Hair like metal strings. Nose round like the ball in His throat.

He's smiling today, teeth all triangles like the Big Bad Wolf.

'Hello there, little lady.'

His voice is deeper than any of ours. It makes the pipes whine.

He stands in the doorway and bends Himself over like a bow pulling back an arrow. Still smiling. His fingers are wrapped round that door frame, covered over in His extra-skins, though I know He'll take them off soon enough.

Funny, 'cause He's all white underneath, just like us. He's got the same belly as Cow. The same knobbly knees as Bee, though His are all grey and hairy. If you look close, though, like I've done, you'll see the bits where His skin is falling off His bones, wrinkling up like an eyelid.

Sometimes, looking at those bits of Him, I wonder if I could kill Him.

He says something else, but I don't understand what it is. I don't reckon He knows I can understand Him most of the time anyway. I ain't never said nothing back. But I get His meaning sure enough. I shuffle myself over there, heels dragging the rest of me behind, and He lets go of the door.

It swings. For one moment, I feel myself a cool breeze. Then the door closes.

The light goes red.

FOUR

He ain't brought me many things from the Outside. The books are three things. And then there was this other time a couple of years back when He brought me some Outside food. It was wrapped up in crinkled armour all shiny and tasting of metal, but as thin as paper. He said it was His 'Lunch'. Said He was giving it to me as a treat 'cause it was my birthday and I was a teenager now.

I din know what those things were, but I took it anyway. It din smell like feed – not like food at all. The armour was all sharp edges, but the Lunch was as soft as Bee's cheeks and covered in white dust, like it'd been dropped on some kind of floor. I looked at Him and I must've looked right suspicious 'cause He started laughing at me and put one of His big hands on my head, all heavy.

'You don't need to look at it like that none, girl. It ain't gonna eat yer.'

It looked mighty alive, skin as white as mine almost, a tongue of something smelling like the in-betweens of Cow's toes poking on out at me. I din know whether to bite it or kiss it.

He grabbed it out my hands and shoved it in His own mouth, yellow teeth chomping down. He pushed just about the whole thing in His mouth in one go, cheeks out, strings of water linking His lips to the Lunch as He took it away.

He handed it to me again, but I watched Him eat His bit down first. He din eat like us. We tip our heads right back and gnash our teeth up real quick so the food don't come out, but His head stayed forward, and the Lunch stayed behind His lips. It din make no crunching noise neither, like feed does. All I heard was His breaths fighting on past the food in His mouth and His jaw knocking like knees.

When He swallowed, the ball in His throat did handstands up and down.

To tell the truth, I weren't so keen on eating it. It smelt funny and I was still wondering if it was alive, even though it din squeal none as He bit it. But, even though Zeb weren't looking over, I could see the Others, eyes out and greedy when they're usually locked on down when He's in. They wanted it, but it weren't for them. It was mine.

I shoved it in my mouth and it was like biting into Cow's belly, all soft. My teeth came together real quick, making my head ring out. My bite din come away easy neither. I had to thrash my head about this way and that, all the dust over my face and itching me, and when it finally came loose I about near choked on it as it made a run for my throat.

It din taste good. It tasted of warm things. Of soft things. Of alive things.

But I chewed it like He did, behind my lips. And the Others were watching that too, and I could see their thoughts.

Looking at my lips. Looking at His lips. Feeling at their own lipless mouth holes.

I swallowed it down, scraping the dust off my tongue by licking the top of my arm.

When I looked up, He was laughing at me.

'You is one weird kid.'

And I guess it was before things turned bad, 'cause I remember snapping my teeth at Him and turning into my corner, thoughts raging hard. I buried myself away and din give no thanks for the gift He brought – He had to take that from me. And He left afterwards still laughing, taking the armour away with Him in a ball, and leaving me with a belly full of hurt.

I wouldn't have done that, though, if I'd known what He was capable of. If I'd known then what the black thing on His belt He called a 'gun' was for, I would've just shut up and thanked Him proper, like I do now.

Things changed. He don't bring me nothing no more.

These days, things are bad. After this visit, I spend a few days in the Outside Inside my Head. I've made a whole bright world in there, all cut from fairy stories. Sometimes it can be mighty hard to calm my thoughts enough to make it real.

Not this time, though. I'm so damn relieved to see that gun on His belt gone with Him that it's easy as beanstalks to get there.

First, you've got to get real quiet. Usually the best way for that is when you're curled up in a ball. You've got to push your face right into the dark, between those knees, hair all around. Then you've got to let your brain get quiet. It takes a while sometimes. You might find yourself chasing thoughts without even realizing that you're following them until you're lost right in them. Pretty soon, though, you'll see those trees and that green come at you, like you're waking up in that place you belong, and it'll get a lot easier to see more and more. Rivers. Rocks. Sometimes even little marks in the sky that I know to be birds – sort of like clouds, but brown and streaky.

On days like these, I can feel the grass between my toes, like tiny fingers tickling me up with giggles. I can feel that sun on my face too, all warm and yellow. And the wind, making my hair stick up behind me.

Sometimes Jack joins me in the Outside Inside my Head, though we don't mention it between the wall. Now I know I ain't never seen him, but in the Outside Inside my Head he looks like Hansel, with curly hair and dots across his cheeks. He sits on a rock and watches me play in the water with the Mermaids, splashing it about. This water ain't like the water in the Tower. It's as blue as the sky and the rain, with little white bits where it snags on the rocks. It feels silky clean.

How long are you going to keep running for, Ele?

He's throwing tiny stones into the water, and it's so smooth that they don't even make a plop.

I ain't running.

I jump out of the water and use both my legs to hoppity-jump over the fairy toadstools to the trees – no running involved, just so we're clear now. I grab the first branch, crackly like scrunched-up paper, and haul myself up, using my feet as a lever, like Jack when he went and climbed that beanstalk.

I know the facts about these things.

Jack, you ever thought about climbing a beanstalk?

Yeah, he hollers back, his voice all small down below as I get higher. *I don't think I'd be any good at it, though.*

You'd be fine.

The branches get thinner as the green gets thicker, but they hold me like I'm an acorn fitting right back on the tree. When I can't go no further, I turn round and look at the shadows on the other side – sometimes dark and sometimes holding other trees, kind of like when your eyes are going back in your head. If I concentrate real hard I can see the long arms of the Willow tree and the spiky hair of the Pine. I can just about see Jack down below, all small, and I wave at him. He waves right back.

The wind feels nice on my face, smelling like Zeb's breath. I run my hands over the paper leaves.

Do you reckon this is what the Outside is really like, Jack?

Isn't it so in the books?

Yeah. It's so.

I can see all the things the books tell me. The Prince, running through the forest. The house of the Three Bears. And even a trail of breadcrumbs leading to the gingerbread house hiding far away in the trees.

I wonder what the Others will make of the Outside. Will they like it once they know it? I bet Bee will. She'll like sitting on the grass and stroking it, reading the words dancing in the air around her. Cow will be fine too, once he gets himself a magic cooking pot and knows it'll get him his next dinner. I'm pretty sure Queenie would still be grumpy even if she was smack bang in the middle of her own fairy story. That's just who she is, ain't no changing that.

I know I'll love the Outside when I'm there.

Ele?

Yeah, Jack.

You should leave.

The Inside, or the Outside Inside my Head?

You can't leave the Inside when you're creeping around in here.

I ain't creeping . . . I rub the paper leaves on my hand.

He ain't listening, though, 'cause his voice is already leaving when he calls back.

You can't escape when you aren't occupying yourself with the facts, Ele.

I drop the paper leaves and start climbing back down the tree and out of my head. Damn Jack, he's always right about these things. Ain't no escaping my bellyache when I'm cooped up in the real, but ain't no escaping Him when I'm curled up away from it neither.

FIVE

I suppose you're wondering what happened when He came in this time. It ain't a good story, so I'll say it quick. There won't be no 'once upon a time' neither, 'cause it ain't just once. It's every seven days.

And just like in 'Rapunzel', there's a Witch in this story. Him. He's as bad a Witch as you ever did see. He came in, pretending to be harmless and all. Making nice to the Princess. Telling her she's pretty. Stroking her hair like Bee does. He weren't as gentle as Bee, though. His fat fingers were all thumbs and got caught up in her tangles.

She din do nothing. Time was when she'd be stroking Him back, trying to get herself more words about how she's pretty as a picture. But she's all froze up beneath those fingers these days. They're gun fingers and they're ready to snap.

He pushed her this way and that. She let Him.

'Where yer gone? Yer disappeared on me?'

His lips scratched her neck as they moved. He had her caught between His legs, one hooked over her like a bar, the other curled round her back. He was all fingers and thumbs over her face, poking them inside her mouth, tasting of floor.

'You ain't still sore about yer brother now, are yer? Yer know why I needed to do it, my girl.'

She can't hear things like that.

He slid His hands round her neck and, calm as, He grabbed the back of her hair tight 'til it was clear her head weren't moving even if it wanted to. So she looked at Him empty, until He pulled so hard her neck screamed out and He got what He wanted.

Yeah. Still here.

He smiled, catching His tongue between His teeth. There were red lines in His eyes like they were bleeding.

'There yer are, my girl.'

He leant in to press His lips up against hers, and He must've felt her twitch away, 'cause something passed over His face for a moment. Some kind of shadow that made His face look as dark as it did *that* day.

Anger.

The Princess's heart kicked. She pushed herself towards Him, put her lips against His scratchy ones and moved them about as He liked it. He was all stiff at first, still thinking His dark thoughts, but they passed. Soon, He let go of her hair and was back to calling her pretty names again, telling her she's His girl.

She don't want to be His girl.

The rest of the story is the same as it always is. I'm hoping one day He'll get tired of telling it. I reckon He does it to prove that He can hurt me if He wants to. But that's where I know He's stupid, 'cause He ain't been able to hurt me doing that since I were a little 'un. He can't get into my mind no more, so there ain't no more hurting to be done. My mind is full of truths and I'm gonna get me that Outside I want like nothing else.

I'm gonna get me it alive, too.

SIX

I wake up when it's still dark and feel Bee hovering over me more than I see her. The red light from the door catches on her eyeballs, making her look like some kind of Witch, and I scream out before I realize it's just her.

'Jeez, Bee, whatcha playing at?'

'Shhh,' she hisses, her breath disappearing like she's looking around for eyes in the dark. 'Don't wake them.'

I look over her shoulder and we're both real quiet for a minute, listening for sounds of them waking up, but really they ain't doing that any time soon. Sometimes I'll wake screaming myself hoarse and they don't even stop their snoring for a second.

'What's wrong?' I whisper.

I can't see her eyes much, but from what I can see they're just about brimming over with worry.

'I wanted to check,' she says, and I know she's stopping to chew on her mouth, 'how you're doing.'

'Fine,' I say right back, but ain't no need to be hiding in the dark. 'Well, no, but I will be.'

The red light blinks as she nods her head. 'I miss you.'

Her words eat right through me. Some of me wants to take her up in my arms and cuddle down with her tight, like we're little 'uns again and nothing matters. But it does. I ain't the Other she wants me to be.

I don't say nothing.

'Tell me, Ele, the one where we came to be here. Inside.'

I roll my eyes. 'Goddamn, Bee, you don't believe in no Outside. You say that it's lies, remember?'

Time ticks on and my arms start hurting where I'm holding myself up.

'It ain't just a story, you know.'

Still she don't say nothing.

'It was Him – the Witch,' I say, with a sigh. 'We all lived happy in the gingerbread house with flowers all around us, and then He came in the night and took us. Just like in the story "Rapunzel", remember?

'We was sleeping. Well, we was pretending we were anyway, but we weren't. He carried us and it was awful cold 'cause it was . . . it was winter.'

And I'm there, in His arms – one under my back and the other under my knees. And I'm kind of sleepy and also kind of scared, but Zeb is there with me so I'm not too afraid. His extra-skins feel all scratchy on my cheek, but I don't want Him to know that I'm awake.

No. That's not right. I do. I want Him to stop and put me down. But I can't tell Him. I can't move. I'm all heavy, and my body has been locked up tight and I can't do nothing.

'And He brought us here to the Tower and locked us up tight for His own. And my hair weren't big enough to be let

29

down, and there weren't no windows anyway. He used the magic door with the flat key that makes the light turn green. And He used His magic to make the food come down and the water rain and the sun bars go on and off. He wants to keep us here forever.'

Bee's breaths are getting all fast. She loves herself a story.

'And how did I get here? And the Others?'

She ain't never asked me that one before. I lick my lips and think real quick.

'You were always here. But we'll get out. We all will.'

Bee don't say nothing to that. I feel her shaking beside me, like she does when I read her the stories with the Giants in. Well, when I used to anyway. We ain't read no story together in so long that I almost forget what it feels like to have her stroke her hands through my hair. I'd read lying down, my head in her lap, and she'd stroke her fingers from the back of my ears all the way to the ends of my hair.

I turn away from her and close my eyes. It ain't fair for her to be over here asking for stories she don't believe in. Stories are truth, and she just sees them as things to pass the time.

She dithers beside me, still shaking. Then, in the quietest of whispers, she says, 'I'm pleased you came to be with us, Ele.'

Then she leans forward and kisses me on the cheek. It's only quick, but enough time for me to feel the soft skin of her nose on my nose, her chin on my ear.

All that badness balled up in my chest melts away.

She scurries back over to the Others to join their pile of sleeping bodies.

I stay up for a while after that, feeling her wetness disappear from my skin slowly, slowly, and thinking of all the ways I'm going to escape with them.

They might not say they believe in the Outside, but I reckon that kiss says otherwise. Bee believes me. She just needs someone brave enough to take her there.

Someone like me.

SEVEN

The sun bars come on in the morning and I'm up and running in my spot with a skip in my step. I don't quite manage to push myself up twice again, but I did it before and nothing really matters today anyway.

The feed comes down and I leap over to the bowl real quick, even before Cow makes it over. I ain't eaten in a few days and I'm about as hungry as a Bear. I get a good load stuffed in my cheeks before I scurry back to my corner to eat it all up in peace.

I try to catch Bee's eye as she eats, but she don't turn round. That's OK, though, 'cause I know. I'm still feeling her kiss on my cheek, like it's burning bright and it's telling me that she believes me.

I set to giving myself a clean-up. The Others are mighty good at using their tongues, but, mine being so small, I usually go over to the water tap and give myself a rub-down. I splash water over my face and down my arms, and it feels mighty good – much better than the rain when it falls, as that burns something awful if you blink it into your eyes. I spend time getting between all my fingers and all my toes 'til I'm near spotless.

We used to be much better at filling our days when we was young. We'd fall about chasing, wrestling and playing games that Queenie always seemed to win no matter what. Our favourite game was called Three Bear Shuffle. We'd all have to lie down sleeping, like we were trying out beds, and then the one who was playing the Bear would turn round and try to gobble us all up. We'd all shuffle around screaming as Queenie got every one of us.

It was fun – all of it. But it weren't real.

Since I stopped playing with them, they've stopped playing together, too. They sit staring at nothing, or fighting about stupid things. Most of the time, though, they'll just be sleeping.

Not me, though. If you ask me, there's plenty of things to be doing around here, one of which is finding all the proof I need of the Outside.

Mornings are spent looking at the text. Reading each book front to back, back to front, upside down, and in all the ways to try to find the secret code that'll get me out of here. Today I try reading every fifth word backwards, but ain't nothing making no sense. Mostly I look at the pictures. There's plenty of those, especially in the fairy-stories book. My favourites are the trees and the house made of gingerbread. The Others are in the book too, in the story about the Goblins. They're scurrying about in the forest at the bottom of the page, looking just like the Others, even down to their knobbly knees and pointed ears.

I'm in there, too. I'm the Princess and Goldilocks and the Peasant Girl. I'm running and swimming and talking to the other Outside People.

Yeah – that comes next. I got to practise my talking. It won't do to go Outside speaking the click-clacking language of the Others. I got to speak how He talks.

I read all the words in the book out loud, just how they're written. Outside-People talk needs a lot of lips and tongue, not like the Others' language, which sounds like feed rattling down pipes in your throat. I can speak Other better than I can speak People, but that's gonna change.

'Once upon a time, there was a Princess who lived in a Tower, and she was alone.'

Queenie starts growling from behind me, so I lower my voice some.

'She spent all day and all night looking out of the window at her Kingdom below.'

The growling is getting louder, but I can't read much quieter. Instead, I turn round, hold the book between us and read off by heart.

'But the Princess had no way down, for the door to the Tower was locked and guarded by a fierce Witch.'

Cow is looking at the book, all wide-eyed like it's the first story he's ever been told, and I can't help but smile. That boy's heard this story so many times he'll be able to read it with his eyes closed just like me, but you wouldn't know it from his face.

Queenie leans over to me, scowling hard. Bee's just trying to keep out of it by facing the wall.

'Meanwhile, a Prince was on a quest hunting Ogres when –'

'Stop talking Witch, Ele.'

Queenie is mighty mad. She sees me speaking like an Outside Person and it makes her remember that I am one.

Her mouth is so open that you can just about see right through into her. My hands are sweating and slipping on the book. Some of me don't like making her like this. But it's the truth, ain't it?

'When he heard the Princess sing.'

'Stop –'

'What's a "sing", Ele?'

Cow's either so wrapped up in the story that he's forgotten what the deal is or he's mighty brave.

I plain ignore Queenie. 'A "sing" is a sound a cooking pot makes, Cow.'

Cow's eyes go wide. 'What's it sound like?'

Now, I don't know the answer to this much, but I've thought about it often enough to be able to deduce. I shuffle myself over to the bowl and scrape at the sides with my hands.

Cow's mouth hangs open. 'How'd the Princess –'

But Queenie pounces right round and holds the top of his ear in her teeth, getting everyone screeching. I drop the book and back myself up against the wall. Cow's hollering and cowering himself into a ball, and it's only when everyone gets quiet that Queenie spits him back out again. Half her face is still cracked up with anger, but I can see her eyes feeling bad for what she just did.

She holds herself high, but her voice shakes. 'We ain't speaking Witch. And we definitely ain't listening to no Witch talk no Witch lies.'

My heartbeat just about fills my ears, making me feel funny.

I ain't no Witch, I think. But I'm feeling too bad at myself to make a noise.

She's still speaking to them, but turns to me to say it. 'Witches want to leave us. Witches tell lies to make you scared. And Witches shoot people in the head.'

I see all that hurt in her. And I feel it in me, too, like I've bitten a poison apple.

Cow's whimpering in the corner, but I can see his ear is fine. I reckon he's whimpering 'cause he's replaying that day back in his head again – seeing that gun go up behind Zeb's big blue eyes, and the whole Tower disappearing in one second of red and sound so loud that we're still hearing it ringing.

I still hear it ringing.

I shuffle back into my corner. I shut myself up.

Bee covers her eyes with her hands. Cow tries to lick his ears. Queenie curls up to sleep.

As I watch them, I think about Queenie. I ain't so good at remembering too far back. It all gets to be bright lights. There was a time, though, when we was all the same size – when I was smaller than now. And it was around this time that Queenie and I were pretty much the same person.

She'd shuffle around after me, copying every little thing I did. If I was eating, she'd be eating. If I was reading, she'd be reading. And if I was crying – and I remember there was an awful lot of crying back then – she'd be right next to me, crying out with those big eyes of hers. We'd play all sorts of games together, and with Bee and Cow too. And we'd all sleep in a pile together.

Not Zeb, though. He ignored them like they weren't even there, sleeping all on his own, keeping to himself. When I was small, I used to pull on his arm so hard to get him to play with me. But all he wanted to do was pound on the door and search for a way Outside.

Queenie knew I loved him more than her. She din understand, though. Zeb was mine, and I was his. It'd always been that way.

When he got taken, I could see her happiness in her eyes like a rotten bruise. She wouldn't have to share me no more. I guess that was what made me say it. That and the hurt ripping at my insides so hard that I'd soon have nothing left inside me but pain.

'I'm getting out too.'

I might as well have shot her clean in the head for the way her face split.

She din believe me at first, but my need grew. It weren't safe in here no more, not without Zeb. And it's what he would've wanted. I know it.

We weren't the same no more. She was an Other, and I was an Outside Person.

I tried to get her to copy me again – to run like I did and speak like the people do in the books. But her little legs weren't made for standing, and she can't speak so good without lips.

One day, she got fed up with it. She took on the role of the Queen of the Tower and banned all talk of the Outside. Anything that weren't Other weren't allowed. Bee and Cow listened to her. The Outside was scary. What happened to Zeb was even more so. Best to pretend all that din exist.

I reckon Queenie thought that would bring me back closer to them. But it din do nothing but push me further away.

I miss her following me around, but not as much as I miss Zeb. That boy was my whole world before he was taken, and it feels awful empty without him.

That's enough thinking, anyway. Sometimes these things are best squeezed down into the pit of your belly where they can't hurt no one. Brains are made for facts, and I'm in the business of finding them.

When the sun bars go out and the Others settle themselves down, I get to knocking. But it ain't to Jack. It's all in the same place, with all my muscles, until my knuckles are wet with what I guess must be blood.

That wall is breaking open for me, though. I know it.

EIGHT

I wake up to the sound of footsteps.

The sun bars are still off. My hands are ringing with pain, but I shove them between my legs and clamp them shut.

Footsteps.

I sit myself up, pressing my back against the wall, and listen as much as my ears let me with all the blood panicking in them.

Ain't no whistling, though. And these footsteps are different from usual. Not one after the other, but a quick step and a dragging and a dull thudding noise.

My heart is matching those footsteps beat for beat.

'Bee?'

No answer.

'Cow?'

Nothing.

'Queenie?'

'Shhhh,' I hear, and I look over to see Queenie's eyes all red in the door light, looking right at it.

'Is it Him?' I say, though more to myself than her.

'Shhhh,' she says again.

The footsteps get louder before they stop, then something thuds into the door.

Silence.

He don't come in the dark. He don't come today.

My mind is racing and all I can think of is the Prince, right atop his steed, all fresh from killing himself some Ogres.

'This is it,' I say, my hands shaking despite being clamped up tight between my legs. 'We're being rescued.'

We hear a beep, and the light goes green. Then I hear it.

'Aw, shit.'

And my whole body turns to water, as there ain't no mistaking that voice. That's Him all right.

He kicks open the door, bringing in a smell real strange, like strong rain. It makes my eyes water, sends Queenie coughing and wakes the Others up, both of them hollering.

'Shut your hole,' He shouts at them, all shadow, as the yellow light behind Him blinds out at us. I look over at the Others in the yellow, and they shut themselves right up, though Cow's looking like he wants to ask a lot of the same questions that I'm having myself.

Why's He here today?

Why's He here in the dark?

Why are the sun bars Outside?

But I shake my head at Cow and he don't move.

'Where are you, you goddamn sonofa–'

He falls into the Tower. The door slams shut behind Him, making the walls shake, and we all get swallowed up into the black.

'Shhhhit.'

His voice sounds strange, like He's forgotten how to talk properly and is sounding out words for the first time.

I open my eyes as wide as they go.

He's stumbling around near the bowl and we hear a big ol' crash as He trips Himself over, cussing loud. I can see the top of His head all green as He tries to haul Himself up again.

Then I blink. I blink again. But it's still the same, no matter how hard or how many times I blink.

Green. The light above the door is *green*.

Trees start flashing about in front of my eyes, too quick to even think about naming them, like I'm falling down and all the leaves are throwing themselves right into my face.

I put my hands on the floor and I lift myself slowly, slowly to my feet.

He's back on His feet too now, cussing some more and swaying His arms about, trying to feel me out. He falls sideways, banging into Jack's wall, and that ringing is back, as that light is green and I got myself a clear path right towards it.

My leg takes a step forward. Then another. And another, and I can hear Him puff Himself over into my corner behind me.

And my arms are out, too, reaching for that green light.

But something catches my eye. Green light in three pairs of eyes, watching me walk right over to the door.

I stop.

I reach out for them, feeling for their bodies in the dark. And all the eyes get wide, wide. I find a hand, I don't know whose. I pull it up as hard and as quiet as I can.

You need to come with me.

The hand wriggles away.

'COME HERE!'

He shouts so loud that I feel His voice rattling around in my body.

I reach for the hand again, searching around blindly, but not finding nothing. Panic starts biting at my ribs.

You need to run. You need to run now.

But it's too late.

I hear a shuffle behind me and fingers on my back, and I'm pulled back so hard by my hair that I'm swung right into my corner again. The breath is pushed out of me.

My legs won't hold me no more and I fall down, scrambling around, hoping to find some air on the floor.

He's laughing to Himself and He gets down on the floor with me and all I can think about is how He's in my space – *my* space – and ain't no way He can do nothing to me here, as where will I go to be on my own if it's smelling of Him?

I scramble up as quick as I can, but He's faster. He clamps a hand round my arm and pulls me right back, dodging my feet as I kick out one, two, three.

He laughs again. 'Stupid slut, stay still. I gotta – I gotta do this, else they'll find you. They will. They'll see you and . . . THEY'LL TAKE ME AWAY. You want that, eh? You wanna know what it's like without me feeding you, you ungrateful little bitch?'

I kick out some more and He's hitting me hard, fists like metal. He lets go of my hair and is scrambling around for something, making more cusses and heavy breaths. Then something clicks on Him and, just like that, the sun bars come on.

My legs stretch. I jump. I'm up and running before I even know what's going on. It's what I do when the sun bars come on: I run.

The Others holler at the light, diving for cover. He's squinting and blinking and trying to hide His head, still cussing away. He don't see me move. He don't see that His gun is just pointing at an empty space now.

BANG.

Noise. Noisenoisenoise. A ringing that turns the whole Tower on its head, and I feel the floor come right up and smack me in the face. Louder. Louder than anything I ever heard.

Everything is red and I'm seeing –

'STUPID GODDAMN –'

Blue eyes go real wide and –

'BITCH! I'LL GET –'

Seeing the red rain down the drain and –

'YOU PUT DOWN.'

Hearing the ringing in my ears. In my eyes and in my nose and in my mouth. And I can't spit the sound out, 'cause I'm screaming so loud that I've forgotten how to breathe and how to swallow and all I'm thinking about is how this happened before.

And then seeing Zeb on the floor. Seeing his red escape down that drain.

I don't feel Him get up from behind me and stumble over to the door. I don't notice the sun bars turn back to black.

I don't hear the Others quiet their hollering. I don't even know where I am until my throat is empty of screams. And even then I don't know, 'cause it looks mighty like I'm caught up in the middle of a pile of Others and I know that can't be right. I don't do that no more.

But it quietens me some. And I guess that's enough for me to finally get around to passing out.

NINE

There's that lady again – the one with the red-lipped smile.

She's got me close to her, but I ain't afraid, 'cause I can smell Zeb behind me. And I can see his hand reaching over my shoulder and fiddling with something gold round the lady's neck.

We're lying down on something spiky. Something green. Zeb's fingers wind the gold round them. I can feel his breathing in my ear, slow and steady.

Then the lady's hands close round Zeb's. And I frown, 'cause I don't remember Zeb's hands ever being that small. She brings his fingers to her mouth and she kisses the top of each of them, one by one. Her lips leave little red marks on his nails.

Red.

I hurl myself awake.

I blink a few times and see that it's dark – about as dark as it gets. I raise my head up and find a leg in my way. I don't think too much about that. I just nudge it to the side and look over to the door.

Light's back on red.

'Ele?'

I close my eyes and sleep again.

45

TEN

Everything is happening quickly, like blinking.

Wake up. Cow in my face, arm in my back. Bodies.
    'Ele? I'm hungry.'
    Closing my eyes again.

Wake up. Water all over me, making me gasp out cold.
    A flash of eyes, all shining red.
    'Goddamn!'
    My voice, I think.
    Then – nothing.

Wake up. Feeling heavy. Hot.
    Hearing a ringing in my ears.
    Making myself go right back to sleep.

Wake up. No bodies. Cold. Dark.
    I sit myself up this time, feeling as bad as I've ever felt. I blink a few times, waiting for the shadows to clear. They don't.

'This is one long night.'

My voice is quiet, like it's broken. I rest my head on my knees and let my blood settle into being upright.

I hear a shuffling noise and one of the Others comes to sit beside me.

'It ain't just one night, Ele.'

Bee.

I squeeze my eyes up. My belly rumbles something awful, like it's chewing itself inside out.

'How long?' I say.

I can hear Bee biting the side of her mouth. 'Two, three days maybe?'

Takes an awful lot not to just go back to sleeping again.

'No food?'

'Nothing.'

'He been back?'

'No.'

'Well, that's something.'

I let my head fall back and find the wall behind me.

'Why?' Her voice is like a whisper, too.

I shrug, my shoulders as heavy as if I was carrying Cow. 'Maybe He's trying to kill us. Maybe He's gone and died Himself.'

I can't help but smile at that, even when it means what it does. He dies, we die. That's always been clear enough. He brings us the light, makes the feed come down, makes the rain happen. Without Him, there's darkness.

'What do we do, Ele?'

I think about it some. Think about the dark and our bellies and the red light above that door. I even think about going back to sleep and letting it all happen.

'Drink,' I say.

And we do. We drink until our bellies hurt. Sucking water right from the tap. At some point, the rain comes down and scares Cow just about to death. Rain feels mighty strange in the dark, like tiny nails dragging at our skin.

Cow ain't doing well without food. I want to say something to him to make it better, but my voice still ain't working properly and I don't know what I should be saying anyway.

I knock to Jack.

Are the sun bars on at yours?

Yes, he says. *They're on.*

And feed – is it coming down?

Yeah.

OK.

I'm sorry.

Ain't your fault.

He knocks me when the sun bars go off, and I tell the Others to sleep. He knocks when they come on again, and I go round waking them up. 'Cept Cow, that is. Poor boy is better off sleeping, the pain he's in from not eating and all.

On what we reckon is the fourth or fifth day, Queenie shuffles over. She don't say nothing at first. We just sit in silence staring at the red above the door.

'Did He get you?' she says finally.

I swallow the ringing in my ears down. 'Nah,' I say. 'He missed.'

She don't say nothing again, and I wonder if she's still mad at me for practising my Outside-People talking the other day. But then I think of all those bodies around me when I woke up, and I count three in my memory.

I want to say I'm sorry, but it don't sound right, even in the dark.

'Why din you go?'

I'm falling asleep when I hear her, so I wonder if I just dreamt it at first. But then I feel Queenie still near me, sitting quiet as can be.

I close my eyes, not that it makes no difference. I think again about that green light. About that clear path I had to it. And about that hand that wiggled away from mine.

''Cause you din come.'

She goes to shuffle back over, but stops for a second before she does.

'You're more stupid than I thought.'

I frown, watching the light shine off the top of her head as she makes her way back over to the other side of the Tower.

ELEVEN

I wake up feeling breathing on my shoulder.

I don't move none at first, thinking it's Bee or Cow come to lie with me again. But this breathing don't feel right.

It's cold.

I've gone and fallen asleep all twisted up in my corner, kind of sitting up, but with my arms hugged round me. My shoulder hurts like it's been pulled real tight. And I groan a bit when I stretch myself out, touching my toes then trying to reach the black sun bars. All the bones in my back start cracking like they're falling apart.

I've not been doing my running since the sun bars stopped lighting up. My body is missing all the moving.

It's still mighty dark, but my eyes are getting better at seeing. I can see clear as day that the Others are sleeping all piled up near the door.

I rub my eyes and turn back to face the wall behind me, running my hand along all the cricks and cracks I know like the back of my hand.

Then I hear a patter. Like when feed drops out of the bowl and on to the floor. For a second, my belly starts rumbling like it thinks it's gonna get a meal, but I tell it that feed ain't never fallen from the sun bars before.

I keep one hand on the wall while the other one is searching the floor, and I guess I come on them both at about the same time, 'cause I put them together in my head right away.

On the floor is a piece of wall. And on the wall is a hole.

There's a hole in the *wall*.

I pull both my hands away quick and tuck them under my arms. My heart is beating faster than it has in five or six long nights, and for a moment I can't even think of anything past all the rushing around in my head.

Shaking something terrible, I take my hands out from under my arms and I find the piece of wall on the floor. It's about as thick as a finger, but not as long, and pointy at the end, like a tooth. I wish I could see it properly, but I can imagine it well enough. I know my walls.

I shuffle up to the wall again and move my hands around it until I find the hole, air blowing through like a breath. I sit myself up, press my ear to it and about near scream out loud when it whispers in my ear.

My heart is going *thumpthumpthump*. I sit back and look as hard as I can at the wall . . . and you can't even see nothing unless you're looking for it really hard, but there it is. Light. Tiny, tiny. But light nonetheless.

I reach across to Jack's wall and feel for the mark I've made from knocking. I feel for breathing. Nothing.

This one ain't on Jack's wall. It's on the wall away from the door – a wall I ain't paid any real attention to before, as it don't knock nor have a door.

But it has this.

I get real close to it again.

'Hello?'

The whispering is all on one breath.

Some kind of Witch. It's not taking no breath in.

I pick up the bit of wall and push it back in, trying to shut it up. It don't seem to fit quite right, though, as other bits of wall start coming away in dust, and I can't help but scream out loud at that.

'What's going on?'

Queenie hisses it from across the room, trying not to wake the Others.

I jump back from the wall, leaving the bit plugged in.

'Ain't nothing!' I sit on my hands, all my insides swishing about my ears. The Tower is filled with my mad beating heart and it's so loud that Queenie is bound to hear it. She'll hear it and then she'll be all teeth.

I squint at the pile of sleeping bodies in the darkness. I can see her squeezing out from under Cow to come see. See what I've done. See what I've found.

I hold my breath.

Then suddenly the whole Tower flashes with white pain that just about splits my head. The Others holler out something terrible.

But I clamp my eyes closed, jump up and start running, like it's just another day.

Even over all the noise, I still hear Jack's knocks.

Sun bars are on.

TWELVE

When that feed comes down, we clamber over ourselves to get it into our mouths.

Soon as it hits my lips, my stomach wants to throw it all back out again. I keep most of it down, though, and Cow goes around eating all of what we don't.

It feels mighty good to be back in the light. It takes a bit for our eyes to feel the same way, though, and we stumble around for a good while with our eyes closed.

The Others nuzzle into me as I shuffle by, and they come over to inspect me for themselves, making sure my head is all in one piece. Ain't one drop of blood on me. Even my knuckles have healed up nice.

I don't say nothing about the hole in the wall. Try not to even think about it.

I spend time looking at the books instead. It feels good to see trees again. Bee reads some out to me. I lie with my head in her lap, thinking about how nice her voice sounds, even though she's reading it in Other. It's still much nicer than mine, which is all cusses and edge. Hers is silky smooth. She'll fit right in on the Outside.

When the sun bars go off again, it takes a while for everyone to settle back down to sleep. But, with full bellies, they get off soon enough.

I keep myself twisted up, feeling for the breathing on my shoulder.

When I know for sure that they're all sleeping, I sit myself up and I unplug the bit of wall. More of it falls out, feeling all strange in my hand, like feed that's been crushed up real small. I poke my finger in and wiggle it about until the wall stops falling out.

I keep my finger in it, feeling the cold breath on the tip.

I want to take it out.

I don't never want to take it out.

I sit there dilly-dallying, the feed in my belly feeling mighty unsettled. Then I lean myself over and stretch out my hand to Jack's wall.

Jack, you awake?

He takes a bit to answer. So long that I have to prop my hand up with the other when it starts feeling tired.

Yeah.

I let out my breath and lick my lips like I'm about to say something.

He gets there first.

Your feed come down?

Yeah.

That's great, Ele. Really great. I was beginning to think –

Jack?

Yeah?

You think a gun could explode a wall?

He takes his time to think about it.

Yeah, I guess it could.

My heart is thumping in my ears.

That's what I thought.

He don't say nothing, like he's waiting for me to get around to telling him. And I want to say it. I do – I want to. But, also, saying it is awful hard for some reason, and the words, they get caught up before they come out.

Jack?

Nothing. He's waiting.

Let me tell you how Zeb died.

THIRTEEN

Zeb knew the truth before I did.

Not at first, though. First, he was just like me. The Inside was our world, and we filled it with games.

We'd see how far we could jump from one side of the Tower to the other. We'd blow bubbles in the water, play at spinning and lie together laughing like Little Pigs over nothing.

But then something changed, around the time the door started opening and He started coming through.

Zeb stopped laughing.

'I don't like it,' Zeb said to me every time that whistling was due to come strolling up to our door. 'He's hurting you real bad.'

'Naw, it ain't too bad, Zeb. It's just His way, is all. Thinks Himself all big and strong, pushing a little 'un like me around. Don't take long and we can get back to doing our things after.'

And when He came I made sure I din go screaming out.

We stopped playing our games, though. All Zeb wanted to talk about was escaping to the Outside. He'd sit listing all the proofs he knew: the books, the door, Him, us. And he became obsessed with finding the next proofs – the ones that would make it real.

He'd be pounding on the door with his fists one day, then not barely moving the next, like he'd disappeared through it already.

On his door-pounding days, he made me exercise with him. As soon as those sun bars came on, we was up and running.

'We'll need to move fast when we escape,' he'd say, holding my legs as I practised my handstands.

I din want to do no exercise. I wanted to go back to playing games again, to when we was happy.

Like a stupid Other, living in lies.

Then, one night, Zeb came over to me in the dark. I felt his breath on my cheek, and at first I thought it was one of the Others. Around this time, we'd always be sleeping in a pile together, but Zeb preferred to sleep by himself.

He was breathing fast, like he'd been up and running before me. I just lie there, listening to his breath.

'We're gonna get Outside tomorrow. I've got a plan.'

He whispered it, like it was a secret. And I should've told him then that I weren't ready to leave. That I din reckon I was brave enough. That we hadn't even found the next proofs. But I was so happy to have him next to me that I din want to spoil it, so I shut up and said nothing.

He slept next to me that night, tucked into me and swinging with me through trees in our dreams. In the morning, he tested out my running skills, looking pleased when I showed him how long I could go without stopping.

Then the whistling started, and I realized that this was it. Everything was gonna change.

I din want it to.

As the Others shuffled into their corner, I grabbed on to Zeb's leg.

'We ain't got enough proofs, Zeb. Let's leave it a while. Let's wait 'til we know what we got to do.'

'We got all the proofs we need,' he said, trying to stop my hands clinging on to him.

I was panicking. Bee's eyes were wide and I was scrabbling about, trying to talk him into stopping, trying to talk him out of what I knew he was gonna do.

'It's too . . . I can't,' I said.

When the whistling was so close that we could hear His breaths on the other side of the door, Zeb reached over and hugged me to him.

'I believe in you, Ele,' he whispered into my hair.

And, when he looked at me, there weren't no sadness no more. It had been clean swept away with excitement.

I let go of him.

And, when that whistling finally came in through the door, He din see no different. Just me, waiting on Him to bring me presents and pretending nothing else was going on.

I played the game. Even though my heart was beating so loud I was sure it was gonna give me away. He told me about His 'shit of a day'. I stroked His silver hair. And I din say nothing when I saw Zeb slowly get up to his feet behind Him. I din even make a sound as Zeb tiptoed over, face all white and shining with something hopeful, then bent over silently and reached out for the magic key.

I held my breath, though.

He keeps the key in a secret hole in His extra-skins, but He'd already taken them off. It weren't no bother for Zeb to reach in with his long fingers and slide the key out.

And I was watching Zeb look to the door and back at me. But he din move towards it. He wiped his hands down his sides – the key still in one – and then reached out to get me.

And his eyes said it all. That it was time. That it was time for me to be brave.

But I wasn't. And something about the way I seized up must've made Him stop talking and sit up.

I knew that was my chance. That, if I ran real fast like I knew I could, there was a chance I could make it to the door with Zeb. That he could use the magic key to open it. That we could escape together.

But I din know that for sure. And not knowing meant I weren't moving. I looked into Zeb's wide, sad eyes, and I did nothing.

Nothing.

He turned and saw Zeb standing over His behind. He cussed and lashed out, standing up real fast. He fumbled for His gun on the side of His belt and brought it down so hard on Zeb's head that the light in his eyes went out. *Click.* Just like that. And, all that time, Zeb din do nothing but look at me, eyes like big buckets of sky, right up until the point when they went out.

The ringing started.

All that sky tipped down the drain with the blood inside his head. And He – He cussed, picking up His magic key. He picked Zeb up and put him over His shoulder. He disappeared the rest of Zeb through the door before I could even say it to him.

I'm sorry.

It's not your fault, Ele. You didn't have the proof.

Jack.

Oh. It is. And it's OK.

I'm ready to escape now.

Jack, I knock. *I've found my proof.*

I take my finger out of the hole in the wall, and I take my first look at the Outside.

FOURTEEN

Now, let me be honest with you — there ain't a whole lot to see. It's not all forests and gingerbread. It's mainly just light, kind of blue-grey, like we really are in a Tower up in the sky, just like Rapunzel.

I try opening my eye real wide, so my eye-hair don't get in the way and fizz it all up. Problem is that it's real small and I'm not used to seeing things through such a tiny hole. I ain't done much squinting in my time and it makes me wish that I had. I could've had mornings when I din run and jump about, but instead focused in real small just for days like this.

What would I be able to see if I could? Mermaids? Fairies? Dragons?

After a while of looking, I start seeing a line. A line where things stop being blue-grey and start being brown-grey, like when the floor stops at the sky in book pictures. And, if that's the floor, then our Tower ain't in the sky after all. It's on the ground.

I don't even need to climb down my own hair to escape. I'm already nearly there.

I sit staring at the Outside 'til the blue-grey starts being yellowy and my eyes are itching with being so sleepy. Jack is knocking to me, asking me what I mean, and what I see, and whether I've gone crazy for real this time. But there ain't nothing but truth blowing in from this hole.

It's been real this whole time. Right on the other side of one of my very own walls.

I'm thinking about this, trying to think past the numb inside of me to where my feelings are kept. I'm thinking so hard, and looking at the light so much, that I don't notice the sun bars come on, or the feed rattling down, or the Others crowding around behind me. Not until one of them taps me on the shoulder and turns me round to look at them.

'What you –'

Cow's words stop in his throat. He stares with the other two at the Outside leaking in through the hole. They look and they look. And I look with them.

Looking with them makes it real. We all stare at it and we wait for it to not be true no more.

But it is. It's proof and there ain't no running from it, no matter what.

The Proof of the Outside – number six: The hole in the wall.

Bee starts first. Low. A whining, like a ringing in my ears. I frown at her, but Cow starts to join. Then Queenie. They get louder, and all together their noise feels like pain in my ribs.

I try shuffling over to them, try to put my hands over their mouths all turned down into sad, but it don't do nothing to stop them.

'Shut your holes.'

They can't hardly hear me over their noise.

My heart hammers. I try plugging the hole in the wall back up, but the bit don't go back in right and it keeps falling out again, shaking in my fingers.

'Shut up!' I shout, but all their pain is spilling out loud.

I throw the wall plug at them and it bounces off the top of Cow's head. He don't even blink.

'SHUT UP! SHUT UP! SHUT UP!'

I cover my ears with my hands. I try to find the bit inside of me that is glad. The bit that's excited. But, with all this noise, all I can think is what they're thinking.

If that's the Outside, then we really have been Inside all this time.

FIFTEEN

Jack's waiting for me in the Outside Inside my Head, sitting on his usual rock. It looks mighty real now, though. The whole place is breathing as sure as I am. I feel it all over my body. I can hear the wind fluttering through the trees. I can smell the armpits of the Ogres as they run through the forest behind me. I can taste the gingerbread house like I'm already eating it.

I got so much buzzing inside of me that I ain't sure what to do with it.

The Outside is real. I have proof.

I squeeze my head between my fists and look at Jack. He looks as calm as can be on his rock.

You're not howling.

Nah, he says, looking at his hands placed on his lap all neat.

Why?

Do you remember when you named us, Ele?

I frown at him, kicking at the grass growing right under my feet. *Ain't we got other stuff to be talking about than that?*

Just tell the story, Ele.

I screw my eyes up. *It was from* The Alphabet Book. *Bee was Bee, 'cause she's so soft and fluffy. Cow was Cow, 'cause he's got the same stupid eyes. Queenie was Queen, 'cause she wants all the shiny for herself. And Zeb was Zebra, 'cause he always had a long face.*

And what were you?

I blink. I'd gone and forgotten that I gave me a name, too. *Ele for Elephant.*

Why?

'Cause I look so different to the Others.

Jack shakes his head. *I think you knew then that you were too big for that Tower.*

I stop kicking the grass and smile. Big, strong Elephant, pounding her way out.

So, what about me? he says.

Jack-in-the-box.

Why?

'Cause one day we're gonna pull your lever and you're gonna spring on out, just like me.

I'm smiling wide now, but he looks away, poking at a bit of rock that's coming loose under him.

I'm not howling, Ele, because I believed you all along, he says all quiet. *And that's OK. I'm Jack-in-the-box.*

I frown. *But, Jack –*

You can't be in the Outside Inside your Head any more, Ele. It's not real.

He steps off the rock and starts walking away. My stomach kicks.

Wait! I call, grabbing him by the arm.

He turns and looks at me all sad, eyes just like Zeb's. *Thank you, Ele, for understanding my knocks.*

Then he does what he ain't never done before – he kisses me on the cheek. Soft, like Bee. But longer. Like he don't want to stop.

I clutch at his arm until the very last second.

Then I open my eyes and he's gone. And even though I know it weren't real, not one bit of it, I feel that kiss on my cheek even longer than I felt Bee's, and a sadness in my chest like he went and took my heart away with him.

SIXTEEN

When I get out of the Outside Inside my Head, the Others have stopped howling. The air is still buzzing with the noise of it, though, and their faces are frozen with sad.

I want to go to each one of them and wipe up a smile, but they're all sitting tall and looking at me like they've been waiting for me to come back to them.

I smile at them myself, not really feeling it. Bee breaks her sad a little, though. Her eyes see mine, and she's happy I'm back in the room, even if her mouth is still turned upside down like a handstand.

I feel like I got to say something.

'I told you I weren't lying.'

It was the wrong thing to say. I know it as soon as the words are out of my mouth, but there ain't no taking them back. Queenie starts growling, so I put up my hands, shuffling myself back to the wall.

'Sorry – I mean – it's OK to be scared. But this don't mean nothing much, really. It's just a hole telling us what we knew to be the truth all along, and, now that we know, we can escape.'

Queenie scoffs, throwing her head back and crossing her arms. I frown at her.

'And just how you gonna escape? Through that tiny hole?'

I follow her eyes to it. Just a fingertip of dull grey light.

'No, I ain't stupid,' I mumble.

'So, what then, Ele?' Cow looks at me like he wants me to tell him a story.

My mind fumbles.

'Well . . . we wait. We wait to be rescued by the Prince, who will ride up on his steed and –'

'There ain't no one coming to rescue you.' Queenie sighs. 'That's what your stupid brother was hoping every time he hammered himself to bits on that door.'

I want to snap at her for calling Zeb stupid, but then there's that word again: brother. Zeb was my brother. Is that a truth?

There's too much going on to think. It's all buzzing with the air and clogging my throat up.

'The books say –'

'He brought the books,' Queenie snaps. 'Course that's what He wants you to think – that, by being a good girl and doing His bidding like the Princess in the stories, you'll be rescued by a handsome Prince and go live happily ever after.'

Her words are cold water down my back.

'I don't think that.'

'Then what do you think, Ele?' Bee's eyes are looking at me, blue like Zeb's. Like sky. Sky that I want like nothing else.

'That . . . maybe . . . we can work together. Escape together.'

Bee's eyes turn grey. She turns away.

Even Cow is rolling his eyes. 'That ain't the story, Ele,' he says. 'That ain't how it works.'

My heart is beating real fast. 'But . . . you have to come with me.'

Queenie leans towards me, her eyes split mad and sad. 'You should've left when you had the chance to, just like Zeb should've done. When you get your chance, you run, Ele.'

My belly kicks up.

'Then this is your chance!' I shout. 'Run with me.'

She just laughs, but her eyes are so sad she might as well still be howling.

'Come with me,' I plead, trying to reach the Others. But they're already turning away.

'That's not the story, Ele,' says Bee.

They pile themselves up in the corner, bodies wrapping tight and not leaving any holes for me this time.

I don't move. I'm still crouched, looking over to the door, their words ringing around my ears like gunshots.

Run.

SEVENTEEN

Sun bars on. Start my running. Feed comes down. Everyone scampers over to be the first at the bowl.

Now, if you was sitting on the top of those black bars criss-crossing themselves under the sun bars, then you might not see nothing different from every other day. *Everything is as normal as can be*, you'd be thinking.

But the truth of the matter is humming inside my hands and making them all shaken up.

Everything is gonna change today.

I din sleep none last night. I was knocking to Jack, asking him to take my mind somewhere nice again, but he's ignoring me or something, 'cause he din knock back all night. I was left instead with nothing but my own damn thoughts and the ghost of his kiss on my cheek.

My head weren't so much a pretty place to live last night. I was trying to make it think of trees and rivers and green stuff, but it was too busy chewing on the other stuff in the Outside, like Ogres and Dragons and Giants. They're all there, waiting for me somewhere in that blue-grey light on the other side of the wall. And, you know, I'm pretty damn strong, but I sure ain't as strong as no Dragon if I ain't even half as strong as Him.

And yeah, there's Him, too. Ain't like I got an open door to be running out of.

What if the Others were right? Rapunzel might have been rescued by a Prince, but she was so old by then that her hair was as long as beanstalks. Mine ain't even as long as I am. How's a Prince supposed to climb up that?

But this ain't Rapunzel's story, is it? This is mine. And if there ain't no Prince running in and slaying the Witch, then that means this Princess has got to do her own damn dirty work herself.

I've got to be strong as a Giant. I've got to grind up His bones.

I ain't scared.

Now the sun bars are on, you'd think that my head would be filled with all the light again, but it ain't. 'Cause it's been about seven days since He last stumbled in.

He's coming today. I know it. And everything is gonna change.

And I know that I been wanting this, but now it's here it don't feel like I wanted it to feel. The Others have gone and ruined it by saying that they ain't coming with me.

What do they know about these things, anyway? They ain't the storyteller – I am. I'm the goddamn Princess, and if I say that they're escaping with me then they are.

The rain comes and I clamp my teeth right down until the cold and the stinging stops, then I shuffle my way over to the middle of the room to check on Zeb's head stain, just like every other day. And, just like all the other days, it's still there. All faint now, but there.

'Zeb,' I say to it real quiet, like it's Zeb himself. 'We're rescuing ourselves today.'

And the curled-up red ain't never looked more like a smile.

Zeb's real smile was beautiful. Not like a crooked line of blood at all, but wide and dimpled. It lit up his eyes like windows showing sky.

I see it, now. Like he's still here smiling.

And I'm still smiling when I lift my head up and see the Others crowded around me. And I keep at it, 'cause everything is gonna be OK. As long as I keep smelling their bodies all around me and feeling their skin – all soft like the underside bit of your arm – on my skin.

I look at Bee and she's looking at me mighty sad and happy at the same time – it's all jumbled up on her face like the rain has smudged her page. And it's the same on Cow's face next to her, and Queenie's next to him.

And I open my mouth to tell them that it's gonna be OK. That I'm writing this story and it's gonna have a happy ending. But I don't even get a sound out before I hear it, real faint at first, like it might be just a wheeze on a breath. But it don't do nothing but get louder.

We all hear it, dipping and turning in the way that it does. We all know that song like He's just singing our names out. Then footsteps, knocking all heavy and out of time to His whistle. The Others' eyes go wide and white.

My heart is getting mighty greedy now. It's beating up out of its cage already and banging around in my throat so I can't hardly breathe. I look over to those Others. They're all eyes.

'Get off going with you,' I say.

They just look at me.

He's getting louder.

'Go on!' I say.

And they do move, but it ain't over to that corner like they've done every other time He's come. They shuffle themselves so they're all behind me, so I can still feel them and smell them and taste them behind me, even though I can't see them no more.

'No.' I say it, but it's just a croak. Truth is, I kind of want them behind me today. It'll be easier to take them with me.

The footsteps stop. The whistling stops. The light above that door goes green.

And it all happens real slow. That door opening. His big ol' body at the door and bringing in all those smells that churn my stomach right up, and He's all hair and glistening skin and shadow.

His fingers are gripping the door and He's both Inside and He's Outside. And I'm trying to summon all the brave in me, like I got an Ogre-killing Prince hidden inside my chest that I've got to call out.

But something's not right. His eyes fix themselves on me, and I feel the anger He's bringing in with Him like hot breath spitting rain in my eyes. I'm trying to stand up and face

Him, but my legs are shaking too much. All I can see is His gun. I stumble up and fall back down.

His fingers slip off the door. His body moves Inside as the door swings all the Outside out. The light above the door clicks red.

He don't take no extra-skins off like usual. He strides – one, two, three, four, five – and He is there at me, gun in His hand, eyes all wet and red and –

He's gonna kill me. Before I can escape, I'm gonna die.

He kneels down in front of me. I try to jump out of the way, but He slides a hand into my hair from the top and gets His fingers tangled in, pulling at it 'til I almost scream out.

He's wheezing hard. He's so close I can see all the dark bits between His teeth. His breathing fogs up my nose like He's stuffing something hot and wet down my throat.

'Yer gonna cost me everything, you know that, girl?'

I ain't listening none. I should nod a 'yes', but all my head is doing is shaking itself side to side and showing Him I don't want that gun nowhere near me.

He pushes it up towards me and I hold my breath in case I smell Zeb's brains on it. He feels me do it. He sees me back to life again and scared. And He smiles.

'You know what it's like to feel like yer up against it, hey? Naw. Naw, course you don't. 'Cause you just sit on your ass all day, eating yerself skinny while I bust my gut trying to keep you, ain't that right?'

I remember to nod this time, but there ain't no moving my head, so I just stare at Him, wide. Then He goes and pushes that gun right in between my lips.

I feel it, cold in my mouth. The metal tastes like blood.

OakWillowBirchSycamore—

'I can end you, girl. Whenever I want. You want me to do that?'

I try to make some noise, but He shoves the gun further down my throat and I don't want to move my tongue in case I set it off.

Ringing. Ringing.

MapleAshPine—

'Why wouldn't I, hey? What you giving me but pain?'

My mind is going in and out of all places. I ain't never been able to speak to Him and ain't no way I'm gonna be able to with a gun in my mouth, and somehow thinking that makes me go real calm. I stop my shaking. Stop grabbing hold of His arm like I'm slipping away. I just look back at Him with His gun in my mouth, and just about dare Him to pull the trigger.

For a minute, I think He's gonna do it. But He don't. He shakes his head, smiles and takes the gun out of my mouth. He lets go of my hair. He lets the gun fall on the floor.

'Naw. You're too pretty to waste, ain't yer?'

And that's when I feel them. I'd forgotten they were even behind me, but they move all together, like they're one thing. Arms hugging my middle, pulling me tight and locking so I can't move. And then long fingers wriggling over my face and around my eyes, hot and soft as anything. And then a mouth, close, blowing a whisper, before more hands clamp over my ears like doors.

'It's time.'

It all happens so fast that I can't even scream at them to stop.

My hands are clenched. I can see pink light through the gaps between their fingers. I can hear the muffled sounds of Him hollering as they hit Him again. And again. And again.

I can feel it, and I can't feel it.

Just my heartbeat and my head are left together and we're banging about on each other, churning with my stomach.

I struggle to get out.

I can't.

Something as flat as pages is being pushed into my hand. It sits nice between the creases of my fingers and thumb, like I was meant to have it there this whole time.

The key.

And then, when my hands are singing and the taste of blood is in my mouth and I think I'm gonna pass out from not breathing, all the hands go all at once.

And I can see again. The sudden light is like the sun bars coming on.

I don't even think about it. My legs are used to doing it anyway.

I run.

I run even though my eyes ain't working yet. I hop over the black shape slumped right in front of me. I don't slide in the hot puddles around it. I run to the door – one, two, three, four, five, six – and I raise my hand up, like I seen Him do a million times before, and I got the key in it, though it looks more red and smudged than it did in His hand, and I'm whacking it hard on the box near the door and hearing the beep that means the light has gone green. I don't look up to see it go green, though. I grip the handle and pull it with all the strength I got left and it comes open easy. Easy. Like it ain't even nothing. Like I been opening doors all my life.

The door is open.

The Outside hits me, cold as rain.

But I don't stop to feel it. I don't sit and look at all the marks on the floor Outside of the door, or think about how it smells like wet on walls. I don't even stop to look behind me at them, 'cause I know they were right. They don't belong in this story.

And I don't look, 'cause it hurts so bad that I know it'd stop me leaving.

And it's time.

I let the door slam shut behind me. I let the key fall out of my hand. And I run.

PART TWO

OUTSIDE

EIGHTEEN

I'm running real fast on a floor made of teeth. It bites at the bottoms of my feet, like no floor I ever did run on before.

And I ain't in my Inside or the Outside Inside my Head. I'm somewhere else. In a long room, all grey, with walls rushing by in a blur and tiny sun bars above me that light me up in spots.

There's another door. I kick it hard. It opens up with a squeal.

The sun bars turn to bright white and I'm running across a page. A page bloodying up my feet.

And then I'm running down a hill, like the Tower really was high up, after all. The hill pushes me to run. Faster.

Run faster.

I can feel pain in my chest like my heart is beat up. I feel cold in my lungs.

I run. For what seems like years, I run.

It's like pelting through water from a tap, but staying all dry. It's like being blown out of a mouth, all cold.

And then I'm seeing shapes and they look kind of like boxes. Big boxes. Grey. And I see the ground under me and it's grey too, all cracked like it's falling apart, with little tufts of brown hair growing from the cracks like fingers out to get me.

I leap.

And, just when my legs are too numb to feel, like I'm just floating in a puddle of grey, I run right into a door on one of those grey boxes. And I pull it open and throw myself through it and –

And then there ain't nothing.

NINETEEN

I wake up. For a moment, I just let myself lie there on the floor, trying to grab hold of the dream that's trickling out of my head like water down the drain.

Was it a good dream? I ain't sure.

I open my eyes a crack and see that the sun bars are already on.

My head feels like it's on too tight and it's squeezing in on itself in time with my heart, slowing my thoughts to drips.

I blink a couple of times. The sun bars are on awful bright. I jump up to my feet and I start my usual morning running and –

Goddamn! I fall back down.

Some Other has gone and bit my feet in the night. I shove them all red and raw into my mouth but spit them out as soon as they get between my lips.

I ain't tasted no feet like it before. Like walls. Like holes in walls. But sharp, too – like Him.

I blink a couple more times, but still can't see a damned thing but light. My head is swimming with different thoughts, and the only one I can really make sense of at all is *Goddamn*.

I wrap my hands over my eyes and try to hear myself over my heart.

Think, Ele. Whatcha thinking?

And then I remember. I remember what I done. I remember that it weren't no dream.

I scream out but it don't sound right. It don't sound like me at all, and I look around me from under my fingers and I see I ain't in the Tower no more. I'm somewhere else, and it all hits me so hard I –

I wake up. It feels like the middle of the night. This time I don't dare open my eyes, let alone move.

I'm shaking. It's awful cold, but that ain't the half of it. The whole world is breathing on me, as if the tap has gone and run out of water and is bursting air out of its pipes.

My nose is so plugged up with smells that none of them are getting through. All together it kind of smells like Him, but not enough to make me think that He's gone and followed me out. It's Him mixed in with something a little like wall, or maybe floor.

It's digging around in my brain and making all these ol' pictures flicker in my head that I swear I ain't never seen in no book before. Of ladies looking kind of like me. Of hands holding mine. And I get this big flash of something that feels almost real. I'm being thrown in the air and hung upside down, and there are long painted fingers tickling me up under my arms and my thighs. And I'm laughing so hard I can't breathe.

It all cracks my head like I'm splitting in two. I scrunch my eyes up tighter and push myself over on to my front, but even that's all strange. I ain't on no floor I've ever felt before. It's flat and smooth, kind of like skin, but cold and hard. Not like the floors in the Tower, which were all scratched up and scarred from us beating around on them. This floor might never have been walked on at all. Why, I might be lying on a page of my very own book.

Something kicks up in my gut.

I let my eyes open slow. It ain't as bright as it was before. My head is still thumping awful bad, and I have to blink a fair few times before I really believe what I'm seeing. A floor. A floor that definitely ain't mine.

I lift my head up and peek out from under my tangles.

I'm Outside.

Well, inside. But not in my Tower. I'm inside some Outside room that I ain't never seen before, and that almost takes my breath clean away. It's bigger than my Tower. Almost double the size, I reckon, though the ceiling is closer in some places and goes up at the middle in a triangle, like someone big is sucking it up from the top. The walls are smooth, too, just like the new floor, but made of folded bits of black metal like flattened-out bars.

But all this space don't matter none, as it's all packed up with so much stuff that I wonder how I managed to get myself from the door all the way to here in the first place. There's all kinds of things about – some of it I even reckon I recognize from out of the books.

I see a table.

Two – no, three – pans.

Chairs all stacked up on each other like someone has been trying to reach the ceiling.

And other stuff I don't have no proper names for, but what we always called 'drinking bowls' and 'extra-skins', all stuffed into shiny black skins with holes in.

Everything is all shadowy and dark, but I can see it all. It's real.

And then there's the stuff I ain't never seen and don't have the faintest clue what to say about. Hair tangled up in knots tied on to the walls. Animals all stuffed up and dead. Round boxes with letters stamped on them saying TEA and SUGAR and BREAD.

It's all piled on top of itself like it's settled down to bed.

My heart is running in circles. Am I trapped Inside again?

I lift my head up even higher and crawl over to the door, all shadowy in the corner. I prop myself up on my elbows and watch wide-eyed as the door blows in and out, like it's sleeping.

It don't look locked. There ain't no light at the top to tell me either way, though. It must be broken or something.

I put my finger out. The door is a lot rougher than the walls and the floor. A lot warmer, too. I hold my breath and I poke it.

The door yawns open and closes again, sucking in the air from Outside and making me roll away from it. I'm breathing like I'm running at my fastest, but I find what looks like a fist-shaped rock and I shuffle back to wedge that door open.

There. *There.* I ain't trapped. There won't never be no more doors stopping me.

I lie down on my back until my heart calms itself.

When I get up again, I open my eyes and right ahead of me is a real-life window. It kind of reminds me of the hole in the wall back in the Tower, but it's open and full of glass, just like all the windows I seen in my books.

'Cept this one is in front of me. It's here. I'm here.

I stumble over there with my eyes squeezed shut. My body hurts something awful, like I've been running non-stop for days. I lean against the glass and feel whispers on my skin.

Breathe. Breathe, they say.

I *am* breathing. I ain't scared.

I know that I might see some bad stuff out there, like Dragons and Ogres and Giants, but I'm brave. I can beat all of them.

I'm an Outside Person. And I'm Outside.

I bite down on my lip, straighten myself up as tall as my broken body will let me, and open my eyes.

TWENTY

I'm looking Outside. Into the real goddamn *Outside*.

First thing to say about it is that it ain't as green as in the books. It ain't green at all, actually. Not one bit.

Everything Outside the window is grey as walls, and I'd think it was inside too, if it wasn't for that big black sky and that moon shining down on me and warming my face.

The moon. Shining. On me.

I smile so wide my teeth feel cold. But I'm feeling that moon – the *real goddamn moon* – on my face, all warm like a kiss. It's a bendy moon – half there, like someone has chewed it and been thoughtful enough to leave some for me.

Ain't nothing as beautiful as no moon.

The sky all around is glowing colours: blue deeper than pictures of sea, with clouds – *clouds!* – that ain't white one bit, but black and blue like they've been tumbling over themselves trying to get near that moon. And I put my hand out, as they look awful soft, but I don't touch nothing but window, which feels all cold and slippery.

Part Two: Outside

There's so much going on in my head that it starts hurting again. But I try to keep my eyes open as long as I can, just staring at the moon and whispering.

We made it, Zeb. We gone and made it Outside.

TWENTY-ONE

That lady is in my dreams again, clear as if I've known her my whole life. I can see the lines around her eyes crinkled up in a smile. And dots all across her nose, like stars pointing the way to red lips.

She's always smiling.

I want to stay in my dream with her, but when I wake up the sun bars are already on full blast and I know I'm late with my running.

Then it hits me. I'm Outside now. This light ain't from no sun bars at all, but the real-life *sun*, shining real bright through the window – no doubt with a big smile on its face, showing off its fiery beard, like in all the pictures in the books.

I jump up to my feet, a skip in my step and my head all full of wonder at the way the light is coming in sideways and not from the top of the ceiling like it did in the Tower. I smile wide and sneak a peek at the real-life sun in all its glory –

FLASH.

My eyes are all bright white for a second and my knees give way. I cry out, my head splitting up like that light was made of broken glass and my eyes are now full of splinters. I push the heels of my hands into my eye sockets, but all I can see is a big black ball bouncing around inside my skull.

The sun. The sun did that. It din have no smile for me. It took one look at me and scratched at my eyes.

I feel around with my eyes closed for some extra-skins, and I throw a big one over the bar at the top of the window. The sun hides itself, thinking about what it's gone and done, and I can open my eyes again – but that black ball is still following me everywhere I look.

I push my back against the wall and try to calm my breathing.

I just got to think, is all. I just got to figure it out.

So the sun ain't smiling. That don't mean nothing. Everyone has their bad days.

But then there's that grey Outside the window. Those walls, where I din see no trees. No Mermaids. No Princes atop white steeds.

What kind of Outside have I gone and escaped into?

I push my hands into the floor, but then remember that it ain't the one I know.

I try knocking out to Jack.

What have I done?

The metal wall just whines.

My stupid lungs are pulling in air like there ain't none. I grip my arms round themselves instead, and close my eyes real tight into myself, 'cause I know me. I know me and I'm there. Beneath all these strange smells and sounds, there's me.

Me. All alone.

I should never have left the Others Inside. I should have dragged them kicking and screaming across that page of teeth to this new place. 'Cause it'd be better in here with them, wouldn't it? What kind of home is an Outside if it ain't got no Others in it?

All the air has melted and it's too slippery to catch. That black ball is bouncing around like crazy now as my eyes look all what way. I cling hold of me, push myself as tight as I can into the corner and breathe.

Breathe.

Breathe, Ele.

The air starts coming back in. And so do the facts.

I'm Outside now. And I don't get scared.

Being Outside means that there's fighting that's gotta be done. I'm gonna have to slay some Dragons, and if the sun's gonna go be the bad guy then I'm gonna have to take it down, too.

How to be an Outside Person – number one: Don't look at no sun.

I write that down in my head, next to all my ol' proofs of the Outside. All my proofs that were as true as I said they were. 'Cause when you're looking for truth – whether that be the truth of the Outside, or the truth about being an Outside Person – it's good to occupy yourself with the facts.

I ain't gonna look at no sun no more. And that's a fact.

I lift my head up and look around. There's a lot of stuff in here that an Outside Person like me could use, come to think of it. I think back to 'Rapunzel' and pick out a big white extra-skin from a box near my corner. I stick my arms in it all what way, trying to make it look right. It don't have no holes for my arms, so I just wrap it round me.

I look down at myself and I reckon I look kind of like a Princess.

How to be an Outside Person – number two: Wear extra-skins.

Now I think of that Prince, and I pick my way across all the stuff until I find myself a sword and a shield.

My sword is long – one end pointy and the other flat and stuck with clumps of dirty hair.

I pick my shield up off a big black tube standing on its side. It's got a handle on the top and is round, just like the shield the Prince had in the stories. The tube kicks out an awful smell when I take my shield off the top, so I move away sharpish.

Now I look like an Outside Person.

How to be an Outside Person – number three: Look like them.

The sun has gone and hidden itself below the horizon. Good job, too. Now that I've got myself a sword, it won't do no good to be messing with me.

I shuffle my broken feet over to the door, with the last of the day's sun leaking in round the edges. I poke the door again. That rock is still keeping it open, just enough for skinny fingers like mine to reach round.

How to be an Outside Person – number four: Go Outside.

I squeeze my eyes closed and I push the door all the way open before I can talk myself out of it. It makes an awful racket, squealing like it ain't never opened before, and I jump right back and let it close on the rock again, panting.

I got me a look outside the door, though. Ain't no Dragons or Ogres waiting for me, just grey floors and a grey wall without no ceiling on the other end.

I lift my shield high and try again, pausing for only a second before pushing that door right open and peering out.

The moon is up there again, shining in a sky that ain't quite dark yet. I give that moon a quick smile, but it don't stay long on my face.

The Outside sounds too quiet, like someone has put their hands over my ears. I reckon I should be hearing the howling of Wolves blowing down Pigs' houses, or the footsteps of Soldiers to match the way my blood is marching itself around my body, but there ain't nothing. All the sound has been sucked out, and it ain't right. I raise my sword higher.

I stick my head out of the door slowly and turn to look at my new place from the Outside. Seems kind of small, somehow. It's made of the same flat black metal on the Outside, too, but all covered in dents and marks.

It's the strangest-looking gingerbread house that I ever did see.

I give it a lick. It tastes of metal, like when you bite on your tongue and make it bleed.

My heart has forgotten that Outside People ain't scared. It's beating up alarms against my ribs.

All the quiet is eating into me now. There ain't no trees, and that's getting to me, too.

I turn to my right and see what I reckon is a house. Ain't like no house I seen in the books, though. It's made of squares all stuck together and has big windows looking at me like dark eyes. And I can see more stuff inside those eyes that I don't like one bit. Not one bit. A big table, meant for a Giant. People on the walls, trapped in squares. I reckon, too, that somewhere in that house is the thing the Giant uses to grind bones to make his bread.

I drop my sword and it makes a huge clatter as it hits the Outside floor. I jump up and back, letting the door slam on the rock behind me. My ears are whooshing with all the noise and I dive back into my new corner, hiding under my shield.

And I know what you're thinking. *What kind of person spends all their whole life wanting to be Outside, then can't stand it none when they are?*

I know. I'm thinking it, too.

TWENTY-TWO

They're in my dreams. All of them.

Bee is playing with my hair, while Cow is trying to read out the words of 'Goldilocks and the Three Bears'. His voice is slow, click-clacking over all the words like he's saying them for the first time. And Queenie. Queenie is lazing against the wall, her long feet crossed over mine.

'And – the – bears – chased – Goldilocks – away – into – the – forest – and – she – was – never – seen – again,' Cow finishes up.

A big smile cracks over his face, pleased as punch that he read the whole thing through himself, though he's read it plenty of times before. But then I see it. The thought sparking up something behind his eyes.

'What?' Bee whispers, spotting it too.

Cow frowns. 'Why'd the Three Bears chase Goldilocks away?'

All three of them look at me. They always do when there are answers to be had. I smile and close my eyes.

''Cause she ain't the same as them, is she? She don't belong in no Bear house. She's a person.'

Queenie grunts and I feel her toes curl round mine. I carry on anyway.

'Just like how I don't belong here with you.'

Bee stops playing with my hair.

I open my eyes, expecting them all to be mighty sad, but Cow just looks confused. 'What you mean, Ele? You do belong here.'

'Naw,' I say, smiling at Cow's simple way of seeing things. 'I ain't looking like you, for one, am I?'

And now Queenie is smiling too. She looks me in the eye and says, 'I'd say you look pretty much the same, yeah.'

And I look down and it's their hands I see. Their knobbly knees and their pot bellies. And I feel at my mouth and don't feel no lips.

I wrench myself up, my head all in a panic. 'Bee?' I say, but it ain't my hair she's playing with. It's my long, pointed ears.

I am an Other. I am them, and they are me.

And I've gone and left them Inside.

TWENTY-THREE

I barely even make it to one handstand when I wake up. And I ain't sure whether it's 'cause my stomach feels as empty as it ever has or 'cause I'm carrying all this worry.

Course I checked myself as soon as I woke up, and I don't look nothing like an Other. I got the same hands and hair that I've always had. But I can't shake that feeling off that I've done something mighty bad by leaving them behind.

I din have no choice, though. Did I?

I feel them clinging to me when I'm running, making my arms and legs feel heavy as Ogre armour. I squeeze my eyes up tight and try to shake them off, spinning round and winding my arms up and back and round, faster and faster. The more I move, the lighter I feel.

The more like *me* I feel.

I'm an Outside Person. And they knew it too, which is why they let me run, just like the Three Bears let Goldilocks run.

They knew it. Jack knew it. Zeb knew it.

And I can't let any of them down.

I can't never let the sad stop me running.

How to be an Outside Person – number five: Don't think about the Inside.

And I know that's gonna be the hardest of all the rules to follow, but I've got to if I'm gonna be a real Outside Person. Even if I feel that Inside pulling at me to follow it back like a trail of bread, I've got to remember that there ain't nothing but a Witch's house at the end of it.

I ain't never going back to Him.

So I've got to forget it, OK? I've got to be an Outside Person, inside and out, like I've been here my whole life and know everything there is to know already.

I pick up my shield, then stride on over to the door, ready to go slay the sun.

How to be an Outside Person – number four: Go Outside.

And that's when I hear them – with my hand pressed against the door and my whole self pushing at me to go on through.

Voices. Outside.

My heart kicks up and I squat down, scurrying back over to the window.

Is it the moon laughing at me with the sun for what it seen of me last night?

I strain my ears real close, trying to make out the words, but it's all just sounding like mumbled mess to me. One thing's for sure, though: that ain't no Other speaking. Other language is all click-clacking in the throat, and this is more like the words He speaks, but different at the same time.

All my blood drains out of me for a moment, and I have to grip the ledge under the window to stop me from falling over.

It ain't Him, though. I won't let it be. He's Inside. Not Outside. Not here.

I stay real quiet, letting my heart beat my blood back to where it should be, before I lift myself up to the window and look out through some of the extra-skins I hung over it. I can see two shapes moving near the Giant's house I saw last night. And shapes near a Giant's house can only mean one thing.

Giants.

My heart has now climbed up between my teeth and I'm biting down on it hard to stop it from making a racket.

One of the Giants is standing still, tall and kind of orange around the head. The other is all dark, moving from left to right. They ain't very big, but you can tell that they're angry at something. I can feel it, even with the window between us.

I look around for my sword, before realizing that I dropped it Outside last night when I was all in a panic.

I gotta be braver than that now. I strain my ears to hear them.

'The sooner ye do it, the better.'

I'm pretty sure that's what it said – the orange Giant. The other one don't say nothing back and they both just stand there for a moment, sizing each other up.

'Fine,' the dark Giant says, and the orange Giant turns and moves into the house, away from what I can see from the window.

One down . . .

The dark Giant kicks something on the floor and I realize that it's my sword. And, as if he heard me thinking too loud, he turns and marches over. Towards the metal box. Towards me.

I ain't even got time to scream.

I hear the squeal of the door as he yanks it open, and before I can do anything but fall down he strides on in and comes face to face with me.

And he ain't like nothing I've ever seen.

TWENTY-FOUR

It ain't no Giant. It's an Outside Person.

It's a boy.

He shouts when he sees me, and I flinch, but I can't move no more than that. I can't take my eyes off him. He's looking at me all round-eyed and slack-jawed, and he's looking to the door like he's about to run away and get the orange Giant. But all I can do is look and look and look.

It's a real-life *boy*. A boy who's nearly a man. He's got skin so dark he could be one of those clouds whispering to the moon last night. He's dressed in extra-skins of all different types – all bright, like he's been coloured in. His fingernails look like moons and they're all trimmed down too. Not like His nails were. They were as long as mine.

His hair is the most interesting, though. His eyebrows are dark, his head hair is dark, and he even has little dark hairs on his arms. And his head hair ain't like no truths in no books. It's all together and bouncy.

And here's the most surprising thing of all: he's looking at me like he's afraid of me. Him – a big ol' boy – is afraid of little ol' me.

I start laughing. I can't help it. It starts coming, then it won't stop – rolling from me like feed from a pipe. I put my hand to my mouth to stop it, but that don't do nothing but make it echo.

He still looks at me, but now he looks more confused than scared. He steps through the door and it squeaks shut on the rock behind him.

'Are you OK?' he asks, his voice deep but soft, like when Bee would cup her hands round her mouth and tell stories.

(I ain't thinking about Bee, though. I ain't.)

I quit with my laughing, though it's hard to do it completely. 'What's funny?'

And I want to say 'you', but I ain't never said no People words to no one but the Others and Zeb before, so I just smile at him instead.

He takes another look towards the door, that worry back in his eyes again. 'So, um . . . why are you in my shed? And, you know . . . naked?'

I look down and see that the extra-skin I put on has slipped off my shoulders, so I pull it back on. And I'm thinking over what he's seeing: me, all hair and bones, skin white as light, just glowing out.

I ain't looking like him one bit.

How to be an Outside Person – number three: Look like them.

I scowl, covering myself up with my hair, my eyes fixed on my toes like they're the most interesting thing going on here – and not that I'm talking to a real-life boy or nothing.

He takes another step forward and I feel him kneeling down next to me, kind of close, but not quite.

'Er . . . should I maybe get someone?'

I glance up at him and see him looking at me, brown eyes as deep as mud, but pointing over towards the door – where the Giant is.

And goddamn, this boy is stupid. Ain't no one in no books speaking with no Giant.

I fix my eyes on him and shake my head big and wide, so even a stupid 'un like him can see that I mean 'no'. *No. Don't tell him I'm here. Don't tell no one I'm here.*

He stops pointing to the door, but he sighs through his teeth.

'Well, you can at least tell me your name.'

I look at him from under my hair. He still looks kind of scared of me, though he's trying not to show it. And it makes me feel brave.

'Ele,' I say. In People. To a *person*.

He smiles a bit then. It's a smile that catches at one corner of his mouth and goes up like a handstand that can't quite get up off the floor. 'So you can talk, then.' He leans back, his shoulders releasing with that breath he was holding.

And he looks better. Less afraid.

How to be an Outside Person – number six: Talk to them.

He smiles wider, easier this time. 'I'm Willow.'

Willow. *Willow.*

I throw myself forward and choke up on question marks. I got all these trees flashing in front of my eyes, and I want to ask him. I want to ask him:

Did you know that Willows are pretty much always next to lakes?

Did you know that Willows are one of the fastest-growing trees in all the Outside?

Do you know where all the Willows are?

But all I can squeeze out are little gasping sounds.

A tree. He's a *tree*.

Finally, I just give up and sit back on my feet, my head still full of wonder and leaves.

Willow cocks his head to the side so the sunlight coming in through the extra-skins on the window goes and flecks his eyes up with gold. 'Can I, um, get you anything?'

Again, he looks at my Princess extra-skin, and my stomach growls at him.

His eyebrows rise. 'Food? You hungry?'

I roll my eyes and he smiles wide again, showing teeth that are bright white and straight as houses. 'I can fetch you some stuff.' He hops up on to his feet and dashes towards the door, all full of life all of a sudden. He stops before he gets there and looks back at me.

'Erm . . . stay there. I'll be back.'

And, with that, he's gone.

I stand up and watch him through the window as he goes to the Giant's house, charging in through the door like it ain't even nothing.

Now, I ain't saying I was wrong about Willow being stupid, but maybe he's a lot braver than I reckoned. The way he charged in after that Giant, he even looked a bit like a Prince.

I pull my hair from my face and smooth down the extra-skin I got on. I'm mighty pleased I chose this one. It's all white and outwards on me, looking just like what a Princess wears. Exactly what an Outside Person should be looking like when they meet a Prince.

And he said something, din he? That Prince. He asked what I was doing in his 'shed'.

I look around my new room, at the triangle ceiling and the metal walls. It's called a shed.

How to be an Outside Person – number seven: Know all the Outside words.

And suddenly I'm thinking of all the other stuff in here that I ain't seen in no book and don't have no words for. And I'm wondering – I'm wondering how I can ask him what they all are when I'm pretending I've been Outside my whole life, but I ain't able to tell him more than my name. All of this is fizzing up in my throat and churning in my head, and it's a relief when I see him bounding back towards me, arms full of stuff, ready to save me from my thoughts.

He comes in with another breath of Outside and walks over to me. There are ropes on the extra-skins round his feet that are jumping about all excited as he walks.

'I raided the kitchen. Some of these went past their use-by date last month. You don't mind, do you?'

He pulls a hook on top of a strange mini-bowl, and as it opens like a creaky door I smell feed, even though the wet slop inside it don't look nothing like it.

I launch myself at him, snatching it out of his hands and not even thinking about how his skin feels like mine even though it's all dark.

He raises his stupid eyebrow, but I don't care one bit. I sit down and shove my fingers into the bowl and then into my mouth as fast as I can. It don't taste right – all mush and no crunch, like it's already been eaten – but I reckon I could be eating just about anything right now and it'd taste like the best thing in the whole damn world.

I finish off one bowl and start on another, this one all chunky and tasting even stranger than His lunch did that time back in the Tower, making my mouth fill with water.

But I finish that bowl and I get on the other. I eat and I eat. And then I lick up the water from the thing he calls a 'cup'. He watches me drink with that eyebrow raised, so I close my eyes tight. I finish as much as I can, then put the cup back down on the floor.

Willow squints at me. 'You're not from around here, are you?'

I think back to my rule about forgetting the Inside and I nod that I am. *Yes, siree. I've been here my whole life.*

'Are you –' He looks quick towards the door and then back at me again. 'Are you in some kind of trouble?'

He's looking at me like he wants answers. I shift from side to side, thinking.

Trouble. Am I in trouble? I ain't in no more trouble here

than I was before, but then there's no saying what that Giant will do if he finds out I'm hiding in here.

Does Willow know something I don't?

I must look mighty worried, 'cause his eyebrows shoot up into his hair.

'Hey,' he says, putting his hand out like he's gonna pat me on the shoulder but then thinks different at the last minute and strokes his own hair instead. 'It's OK, you know. You're safe here. And I – I'll look after you.'

He says it all nervous, like he don't really believe it himself, but my smile goes wide.

A Prince. Looking after me.

Now, I ain't saying that I need no looking after. I've done a mighty fine job of looking after myself until now. I din need no Prince to escape that Tower, did I? But there's no harm in having a Giant-slayer on your side. Especially when you're living next door to one.

He looks at my smile and his shoulders rise. 'Yeah,' he says, nodding. 'I can look after you.'

He believes it this time. I can tell.

'I've done it before . . .' His eyes have gone sparkly and, even though they're looking at me, they ain't really. They're looking backwards, to an Outside Inside his Head. I get up on to my knees to peer in with him.

My movement snaps him back out and his face starts turning red. 'Um,' he says, moving back. 'OK. This is going to sound pure weird.'

He starts tapping out words on his knees like he's got a

Jack living in there. 'Don't laugh, OK?' he says, raising his head to check that I ain't laughing, before smiling back down at the floor and tapping on his knees even faster.

I sit back and lick up some more water to make sure I ain't got no room to laugh.

'All this – you being in the shed and being –' he eyes me guiltily – 'you know. It just kind of reminds me of this game I used to play when I was a wee kid.'

He waits for me to laugh, but he ain't said nothing funny yet. He carries on.

'I had this, er, imaginary friend.' His cheeks go even redder. 'Called Angus. He was a time-traveller – in the game, I mean. And he'd turn up at the bottom of the garden – the bit behind that broken dyke. Aye, well . . . he'd turn up there, you see, and he'd need me to take care of him, right? 'Cause he'd just come from, I don't know, Ancient Egypt or something, and he'd be hungry and need a rest and stuff. And I'd help him.'

He's smiling now, lost in his story, and I kind of like it. Even though I don't know what no time-traveller is or where in the Outside Ancient Egypt is. It don't really matter none, 'cause it's a story and it's his.

'I think he took me with him sometimes, too. Yeah, he did. I remember us playing this one concert with Mozart, right, and –' He catches my eye and coughs, the story disappearing from his eyes. 'I know it's stupid. But it's kind of the same as this, right? Like you're Angus in real life. And I'm bringing you food . . .'

I nod, 'cause I know that stories can come to real life. I know it right now.

He shakes his head. 'I can't believe I just told you that. I've not thought about Angus since . . .' His eyes flash with something dark, so quick that you might not see it if you weren't used to seeing shadow. He sees me looking and forces out a smile, bringing out a pile of extra-skins he's gone and got with the food. 'I brought these. They are – were – my mum's.' He swallows.

He hands me some extra-skins for the legs and other things I can't make out what they're for. But he's looking at me, so I nod at him thanks.

He keeps on looking, then seems to get real awkward, like he's caught himself doing something he shouldn't. He turns round and looks right to the door. I wonder if he's gonna go marching back out again, so I shout out.

'I'm not leaving,' he calls over his shoulder. 'Put them on so I can turn round again.'

I look at all the extra-skins in my hands. Put *these* on? My heart is beating real fast. I don't fancy making myself look like I don't know what I'm doing. He's saying 'put them on' like it's something I should know, and I don't want him thinking I ain't no girl of the Outside.

I try putting them on any way I can.

'OK?'

I don't say nothing, but I guess he thinks it's OK, 'cause he turns round and looks at me.

And he laughs. It starts out all small, but it gets bigger and bigger.

My teeth want to jump up and bite him to teach him some manners, but I don't.

How to be an Outside Person – number eight: Don't bite people.

'Are you serious?' He must see that I'm mighty serious, as he quits his laughing soon enough. 'They're underpants, Ele. Not a hat.'

Well, if you ask me, the idea of putting on extra-skins and having different names for it all is stupid. I throw the 'underpants' right at him, hard as I can, and they land at his feet.

Ain't no one need to be good at throwing underpants, anyway.

And he's still laughing with those big, stupid eyes of his, so I pull myself under my hair and sink down into the floor.

I can't believe I ever thought he'd look after me. Laughing at people ain't looking after.

'Are you seriously telling me you haven't seen underpants before?' He's looking at me like he both wants an answer and he don't, so I keep on being mad in silence.

He shakes his head of thoughts. 'They're for . . . you know, for your legs and stuff.' And he takes up the pink underpants and he steps through the holes at the bottom, even though his feet are all big and he's getting them dirty. He pulls the underpants up to the top so he's trapped in them.

I look at him. I look at the underpants. And I realize I was right. He *is* stupid.

I close my eyes, my thoughts raging, 'cause it's like being back Inside again. Here I am – an Outside Person Outside – and he don't believe that I belong here neither.

He thinks it's *funny*.

Ain't no one allowed to laugh at me and tell me I'm wrong. I'm in the proof-finding business and I say that *he's* wrong. I ain't never seen no one looking like him in any book I ever read – not one of them.

It's him that don't belong here.

I curl up away from him.

He starts poking me in the back. His finger's all stubby and wide, not like any of the Others poking me.

'Ele? Come on. I'm sorry. I didn't mean to laugh. But you did have pants on your head. You get that that's funny, right?'

I scowl, and curl myself up tighter.

'Ele? Come on. Talk to me. Tell me where you're from.'

He pokes me again, but I don't say nothing. He don't neither. I can feel him fidgeting, though, tapping on his knees and trying to see my face in between my hair.

After a while, he starts being still. And I must be awful tired or something, as it don't take long before I drift off to sleep.

TWENTY-FIVE

'She was always covered in paint. Mainly greens. Dad nearly had a fit when he came back one night and saw what she'd done to my bedroom wall. Ha! Trees again, of course. She was always painting trees.'

I hear him as I'm drifting in and out of sleep. He's telling me things about himself. About things as they are. About someone called 'Mum'. He's telling me more and more about her as he's talking, and moving closer to me, too. His voice sounds right nice and clears some of the badness out my head.

Trees.

'I remember, this one time she'd tried painting this big tree from memory, but she'd started too big. All the branches were on and it looked like she'd need to throw out the whole canvas. But she didn't – maybe 'cause they're expensive. She just kept painting right off the canvas, right into the air. Huh. I'd forgotten about that . . .'

He don't say nothing for a long time.

'I don't remember when it was that she stopped. I guess it wouldn't have been too long before, you know . . . She wouldn't have stopped lightly. But she did get bad. By the end I mean. I don't know. Maybe I can't remember.'

I hear him shuffling around like he's poking something in something else. It's mighty annoying.

'That and . . . and I wasn't there at the end. I'd gone to school – I was only eleven – and, when I came back, there were all these people in the house. And I saw Dad – saw the state he was in – but I still asked. I still made him say, "She died, Willow." I remember he said it just like that. "She died".'

Died. Zeb's eyes going all wide. It rips up from my belly and starts flickering in front of my eyes. His hand stretching out towards mine. His blood.

I clutch myself real hard, and I guess the movement makes Willow remember just where he is, as he sniffs.

'Agh, don't know why I'm saying all this stuff, anyway.'

I stay on the floor, trying to push down that feeling like the sun has somehow got into my chest and is burning me up from inside to out.

'Guess it's all this junk. It does get you thinking, hey?'

I get up slowly, still hiding my face. And I sit like him, all creased up.

'Why'd she die?'

I say it real quiet, using my People words.

I reckon he din hear me at first, as he don't say nothing until: 'Brain tumour.'

I nod, like I know exactly what that is. Willow watches me out of the corner of his eye, rubbing his nose on his sleeve.

How to be an Outside Person – number nine: Know someone who's died.

'Zeb died, too,' I blurt out quick before I can stop myself. I lift my head up to look in his eyes. They're all red round the edges.

'Zeb?' he says. 'Someone you knew?'

I nod. I try to say the words, but they ain't coming out right now. They're all jumbled with Other.

And I start seeing it happen again. The gun coming down. His eyes looking at me wide. Looking and seeing me. Knowing it's all my fault.

Willow puts his arm round me – all nervous like he ain't never touched another person – but, as soon as his arm touches mine, I shove my head into his chest and pull him close, smell the Outside on his clothes, and it feels better somehow. Like Zeb's back with me.

He stiffens up like a wall at first, but then starts moving his arm up and down my back in a way that's real careful and nice. Then he starts loosening up a bit, even though I can hear his heart busting at the seams through his chest.

'I'm sorry,' he says.

And it's OK, 'cause he's there. And that's OK.

He starts speaking some more then – telling me all about himself and his life Outside like he ain't never spoke to no one neither. It reminds me of the time Zeb stuffed a load of feed up into the tap and then turned it on to see what would happen. It was all still at first, but you could feel something building up and up, until finally all that water came whooshing out all at once and the feed was thrown right across the other side of the Tower.

Not that I'm thinking of Inside or nothing. It's just all this 'junk', ain't it? It gets you thinking.

He tells me about something called 'music practice' and 'hanging out'. He tells me it's all boring – all the things called 'school' and 'chores' – but it don't sound boring to me. I don't reckon I understand a lot of it, but it feels nice listening to him tell his stories. I have my ear pressed up on his chest and I can feel his voice inside my head like it's my own.

I know so many words.

'Hey, you want to see one of my mum's paintings? There's one in here somewhere.'

He don't wait for me to say nothing. He gets himself up quick and dodges his way through all the stuff in the shed, cussing as he knocks things and sends them wobbling.

'Here it is!'

He half pulls something flat out from behind a big brown box with doors. His eyes are dancing about like he's right excited and also a bit pissed off that whatever a 'painting' is ain't coming out quite as easy as he'd like.

I kneel up straighter, to watch him struggle. When he finally pulls it loose he takes a moment to look at it all to himself before he brings it over, dodging all the stuff in his way with the painting above his head like his own ceiling. He kicks at the stuff in his way like it all don't matter.

He's breathing hard when he gets over to me. He falls to his knees, twirling round the 'painting' so it's looking at me and –

Green. So much green.

Trees, too, like nothing I never saw in the books. As big as me.

I shout out loud, leaning over to touch their leaves, but Willow pulls the painting away.

'Er, best to just look, you know. Fingers and all.'

Looking is still the best. There are trees all big at the front and trees going back, too, like I'm sitting on a hill looking out through a window. I saw pictures of trees before in the books, but never as big as this. And it ain't even that this painting is very good or real, like the trees in *An Encyclopaedia of British Trees*. These trees are all a rush of colour – colour rubbed on like it was done with fingers. And I look at all the greens and it's like every leaf is inside me like a feeling.

'Sycamore,' I say, pointing at the tree in the corner. 'Elm.' And I'm looking at the one at the bottom, as I can't tell if it's a Birch or a baby Oak.

'Birch,' I say finally. And I point to the ones in the background. 'Pine.'

'Jeez, you know your trees.'

I sneak a peek at him and see that he's looking mighty impressed, like he should.

I lift my chin and straighten up. 'Willow,' I say, pointing to the leaves hanging down in the corner.

His eyes go wide, and he moves in to look closer. 'Willow . . .' he whispers. 'Huh. I never really thought of me being a tree.'

That's 'cause he's stupid, but I don't say it out loud.

There's something else in the bottom corner. A word: *Ashley*.

'Ash,' I say, pointing to a sprout just above the letters.

'Ash? As in Ashley?' Willow picks the painting up. 'That was Mum's name.'

Now, I don't know why no one needs two names, but it don't seem the time to ask.

'You're sure?' he says, still looking at the little sprout on the painting. 'You're sure it's an Ash?'

I don't know if it is an Ash. And I don't know whether I should be lying about something as important as that. But, when I see his smile when I nod, I reckon the lie was worth it.

TWENTY-SIX

By the time Willow leaves the shed, the sun is bleeding right out across the sky.

I watch from the window as its red trickles down the drain of the horizon, and I'm wondering if Willow is gone forever now, just like Zeb was when He took him out of the Tower.

Willow said he'd be back soon, though. And I think I believe him.

I'm thinking back on all the Outside words I learnt today, like underpants – which I managed to put on in the end like it weren't nothing, like I was an underpant-wearing natural. Willow even said they looked better on me than they did on him, before going as red as an apple.

He's a strange 'un, but I like him.

I drink another big gulp of water, trying to use my lips instead of my tongue this time, just like Willow does. I get some down my nice new 'dress', which is the same type of green as a Fir tree. The cold feels nice on my chest. I din realize I was getting so hot.

A shadow passes over my insides, making me feel awful funny. I sit down and drink some more water. I've been standing up too long, is all. I'll just close my eyes for a bit, 'til Willow comes back, then I'll take him on some adventures. We'll go play with Mozart and fight Ogres in Ancient Egypt.

He'd like that. I know it.

TWENTY-SEVEN

I'm remembering Him. I ain't supposed to, and I don't want to neither. But I can't stop it.

He's out of His extra-skins and lying on the floor all stretched out, like it's His. I can smell Him in the back of my throat, all sweat and dirt. He has my head locked in His arm and I can feel the heat of His dirty ol' armpit on the back of my neck.

It's difficult to breathe proper, so I do it slowly, thinking it through. I watch the bones in my chest, each one like a finger, as they clench and unclench. In and out. I got this.

His breathing is slow, too. I'd think Him asleep if I couldn't feel the muscles in His arm working to keep me held.

He don't say nothing. I don't make no sound neither.

We lie like this for hours, Him occasionally moving to scratch the tangles on His chest. Sometimes I need to swallow. I do it slow, but He feels it every time and makes it tighter.

Then – just like that – He lets go.

The air all rushes in at me and I'm trying not to cough it out. I roll over to my front and hide my face from Him.

I hear Him getting His extra-skins back on again. I hear Him walking over to that door. Then the beep.

He don't say nothing as He leaves. The door slams.

I wake up all in darkness. I'd think I was dead if I weren't feeling so much hot all over my skin, like I'm burning right up. I shove all the stuff off me, but it ain't no use. I groan out loud, and look deep into the dark for something, 'cause I don't know where I am, and all I can see is colour bubbling at the edges of shapes I don't recognize, and I'm trying to shove all the stuff off me, but I already did, din I? I'm too hot, but it's too dark to be sun, and I throw myself over to the water – *waterwaterwater* – and the ground hits me like His fist and I'm too far gone to be closing my legs. I scream out, thrash my arms about to ward Him off and they knock the water over.

I pull myself over to it on the floor, a puddle like a window right into another dark world, and I push my face in it. My tongue don't wanna come out of my face – it's so thick and dry. It don't help. It don't.

I cry out. Thrash. Try to breathe in. Can't.

Ele, I hear. *Ele*.

And I think, *Zeb, is that you?*

It's time. Time to escape.

TWENTY-EIGHT

Voices. Voices are talking. And I'm on a cloud.

I'm dreaming about Jack – the one in the stories. I'm thinking of his beanstalk, how it grew from the ground. His own tree. It took him right up into the sky and into all those clouds. And I'm thinking that it'd be mighty hot up there, as there wouldn't be no place to hide from the sun.

I'm up there. On a beanstalk. Mighty hot.

'How long are we talking?'

'Not long.'

'How long?'

'Two days, I think, but –'

'Two days!' Hissing. 'Yer a fool, Will.'

Mumbling. 'Come on, Dad. You didn't even notice! If I hadn't come –'

'What if she's listed as missing? There'd be all sorts around then – police, doctors, press. Nae. Ah won't have it.'

'She's not missing! I told you. She's just a lass from school who needs a place to stay –'

'Aye, but that place isnae a shed, Will.' Hands scratching

through hair. 'Why ye didnae tell me . . . Why haven't ah seen her before if she goes tae yer school?'

A grumble. 'She's new. She's not from here originally.'

'Aye, well . . .'

There's moving around me. Someone big is pacing up and down. The footsteps rumble me like Giants.

Giants. *Giants.*

I call out, but it all sounds wrong. Like moaning.

I ain't scared. I ain't.

'Ele?'

Willow. Willow is here, I can smell him. I flail out, hold his arm. My clouds start spinning round and round.

I'm gonna fall.

Hands holding mine. They've got me.

'Willow.'

They've got me.

'Is she OK?'

'She's just got a cold. She just – she needs me to look after her, OK?'

'Aye, well, I'll go and get –'

Willow sighs. 'I've got this, Dad! We don't need you.'

Silence.

'Ah see.'

'Dad, I didn't mean –' Willow tries to leave, but I clutch him back to me.

Footsteps. Giant is leaving. Willow is fighting it off.

I open my eyes and everything is all blurry, but I see Willow there above me. He's leaning over me like I'm Sleeping Beauty and he's come to wake me up.

'Willow?'

He holds my hand tight, like he ain't never letting me go.

'I'm here,' he says. 'I've got you.'

He's got me.

TWENTY-NINE

I'm feeling mighty rough when I wake up again, like a whole world is sitting inside my head. There's a strange light coming through my eyelids and a smell like old things.

I squint out. It's bright, but kind of like something white is covering up the sun.

Where am I?

Something about clouds?

I move my arm up, but it don't feel like it belongs to me. It feels pumped full of water and it slaps down on to my face.

I'm mighty hot.

Groaning. I'm trying to keep quiet, but my throat is making a noise all on its own.

I look out through my fingers. I'm under something. Something heavy, smelling like the extra-skins in the shed. It's trapping me on the cloud.

Am I being swallowed?

Right down, by the sun. Its lips burn. There's a humming coming from somewhere. And a clicking, all out of time to my heartbeat.

I move my tongue over my teeth and taste something so bad that I turn over and puke my guts up. It all hits what sounds like a feed bowl someone has gone and put next to me in the night.

'You're awake.'

Willow.

I catch my breath. Wipe my mouth. Turn to him. He looks all shadow.

'Where?' My voice is dry as wall.

'My room. Inside the house.'

Something grips my stomach tight and I sit up straight without even thinking.

The house. Inside the house.

Where the Giant lives.

My ears are ringing as I take in all the shapes around me, all bright. The boxes standing tall in the corner, dribbling out dresses like they're dreaming. The grey door, closed.

'Whoa, slow down.' He pushes me back with a hand on my shoulder. 'It's fine. You're on my bed in my bedroom, OK? I've cleaned you up and got you some blankets.' He hands me the heavy thing that was lying over me. 'You're safe.'

'Blankets'. 'Bed'.

He keeps his hand on my shoulder until I calm myself down.

I squint. 'Bright.'

'Oh, sorry.' He stumbles over a table, and all kind of shapes and stuff goes rattling as he climbs on to it. 'I'll close the blinds.'

There's a rolling noise and it's like he's made the sun go down. My eyes sigh and relax right into where they're supposed to be again.

I lie back and feel something soft and warm behind me. For a moment, I think I've gone and sat back on some Others, before I turn and see squares of clouds bagged up in coloured stripes. And then I realize I'm lying on a big one of them, too, not no cloud on no beanstalk. When I move, I bounce – up and down – like I'm jumping. It makes me feel mighty sick again, though, so I stop sharpish.

Bed. Like the one Goldilocks slept on before the Three Bears found her.

I look up at Willow. 'You told him I was here?'

He glances at me from between his fingers. 'I know. I'm sorry. But I came in to check on you and you were in this big state – you didn't even know who I was and you were burning up, and . . . well, I couldn't just leave you there, could I?'

I slide myself further down under the blanket, until I'm hiding my face. It's dark in here.

'The Giant. He's mad.'

'Giant? What – Dad?'

I peek up at him.

Willow shakes his head. 'He's not mad. He's just not used to seeing people in the house, is all. He likes being alone out here.'

I frown. 'Alone?'

'Look,' he says, sitting down on the bed next to me so it tips me towards him. 'You don't have to worry about him telling anyone you're here – if that's what you're worried about. I told him that I know you from school anyway, but Dad, well, you wouldn't see him messing around in someone else's business. It's just . . . not him.' Something dark passes over Willow's face. 'He isn't even that interested in mine, let alone –' He shakes his head.

'Alone,' I say again.

I'd never thought about Giants being alone. They're all angry in the books, screaming about killing and everything. But, now I think about it, they're kind of alone, too, just like the Princess in her Tower.

I look towards the door, listening for him.

'The Giant. He's here?' I say.

Willow nods, biting his lip. 'He doesn't need to come in, you know. I'm looking after you fine.'

I've started shaking.

'Even Giants shouldn't be alone,' I mutter. I pull the blanket over me 'til I'm trapped in tight.

I'm ready, and I ain't scared.

OakWillowBirchSycamore.

Willow nods slowly and goes over to the door, looking back like he's gonna say something, but then shaking the words from his head again. He opens the door and I'm almost expecting Him. Him all big and dark and Him.

But it ain't Him.

It's the orange Giant I saw through the window back in the shed, but he ain't nearly as tall as they make out in the books – only a little nearer the ceiling than Willow. He's much bigger round the middle, though, with shoulders so wide he might be wearing armour under his brown extra-skins.

I'm expecting him to look all angry, but he looks mighty uncomfortable, dallying about on the spot in the same way Willow does when he's nervous. He couldn't look less like Willow if he tried, though. He has the same pale skin as me. Orange hair is fuzzing off his head and face in all directions, making him look like a smudged sun. Even his eyes would be covered by the fuzz if they weren't so wide and brown. His nose is the same as Willow's, though – kind of flat with big wide nostrils that are smelling all the smells in the room.

He mumbles something and his voice is even deeper than His was, kind of like the feeling of the wall when Jack is knocking. It rumbles in my ears.

He looks at me all serious, licking his lips, hands scratching through his face hair.

And he comes in, one foot at a time, like I'm some kind of monster and he's worried that I'm gonna throw him right off the beanstalk. The closer he gets, the more I see of the lines round his eyes, the white bits hiding in his hair. And his big ol' hands all cracked up with dark lines and black fingernails.

I ain't shaking no more. He stays near my feet, but Willow comes and stands right next to me. Willow and me are staring him down, and he squints into our looks like we're shining something bright.

'Hello,' I say, 'cause all this silence is making me want to laugh.

His nostrils flare even wider, and he throws a look to Willow. 'Yer American?' he says.

He has the same strange way of talking that Willow does, but he's even harder to understand. I ain't sure what 'American' is, so I just smile at him.

He looks at me all nervous, which makes me want to laugh even more. A Giant, scared of a little thing like me.

I ain't sure what to say next. Fair to say that I ain't got much experience when it comes to meeting Giants. Feels like someone's got to say something soon, though, as all the words we're not saying are making this place awful stuffy.

'Thank you,' I say eventually, hoping he'll know what for and all.

He darts a look at Willow. At the floor. At me again. Then he nods, once, quick. 'Yer . . . yer feeling better?'

I nod back. Everyone is nodding their heads up and down like they're floating about.

I glance up to Willow, who rolls his eyes.

'Well,' the Giant says, voice all booming. 'Um.' He looks around again, as if all the objects in the room are telling him what to say and he don't know which one to listen to. He shakes his head. 'Will should've invited ye in sooner. The thought of ye in that bloody shed –'

'Dad.' Willow jumps in.

'Aye,' he says, nodding. 'Aye.'

The silence is creeping back again, so my mouth starts speaking all on its own, just to fill it. 'I'm Ele.'

'Ezra.'

Ezra.

My head explodes with all sorts of questions and I dig through them for the right words.

'Not "Dad"?'

Willow laughs and I pull some more blanket over me, looking hard at the pattern on the top. It's all criss-cross and stripes, like a multi-coloured zebra from *The Alphabet Book*.

Ezra-Dad shifts from foot to foot. 'Ye don't have the word "dad" where yer from?'

I bite my lip to stop all the thoughts racing out of my mouth at once.

Which rule is the right one?

'There's some words that are different,' I say eventually.

Willow smiles, putting his hand on my shoulder. 'I'll teach you them.'

My insides light up.

Ezra-Dad looks between us and moves to the door like he's carrying a load of stuff on his back. He stops before he leaves, though, hand scratching the door frame. 'Yer welcome tae stay. Long as ye need.'

He leaves without waiting for me to gather my words up, and he's all the way out of the door before I manage to shove another 'thank you' out of my mouth.

How to be an Outside Person – number ten: Be nice to Giants.

Willow stares after him, mouth open wide. 'Well, that's a first.' He looks down at me, smiling, and the lines on his head crease up. 'Looks like you've made quite the impression.'

We look at each other. I'm hoping he's gonna stay and start explaining some of the stuff that's in his room, but he nods, kind of like Ezra-Dad, and moves himself towards the door, too.

'You coming back?' I shout, as he opens it.

He turns, seeing me all concerned. And he flashes me a smile. 'Yeah, course.' He goes to close the door behind him.

'Leave it open!' I call.

He shrugs and pushes the door wide again, before disappearing down under the floor, bit by bit. The door tries to close itself, but it ain't strong enough to go all the way.

It's open.

I can leave whenever I want.

THIRTY

The lady with the red lips is pressing something against my head. It feels cool, nice. Things are blurry, but I see her lips. I see them saying something to me. I can't hear what the words are, but it don't matter.

She's tucked me into something warm and I feel safe. I feel toes wriggling against my toes and see Zeb tucked in from the other end.

And then the sound turns up. Just for a second.

'Snug as a bug in a rug.'

I jolt awake.

'Whoa!' Willow says, jumping backwards to stop my head from cracking into his. 'It's OK.'

I try to get up and start my running, but Willow pushes me back down. He's got something in his hand – some kind of pink square that's dripping water.

'You still have a temperature,' he says, putting the square on my head so the water dribbles down into my ears. 'I brought you a flannel.'

I rub my eyes. There's a sun ball above my head that's shining yellow light on all the room. I want to go back to sleep, but Willow is dithering from one foot to the other, looking like it's time to get running after all.

I groan.

'I have a surprise for you.'

Books.

I jolt up again, so the flannel falls off me and slaps into my lap. I wipe the water off my head, looking around for them. But all I see is a black box shaped like a keyhole that Willow is holding to him like it's a Golden Goose.

'What's that?'

'This?' He's looking excited, so I start getting excited, too. 'I thought I'd show you it. I don't know what you're going to make of it, though . . . You've got to promise not to laugh, OK? It's, you know, important.'

I nod as he unclasps the metal bits on the side. I strain over myself to see it, but he's still rabbiting on.

'It's just, like, it means a lot to me, you know? And I guess it doesn't really matter what you think, but I kind of want you to like it.'

I nod again, but he still ain't opening it.

'Not that it matters if –'

'Just open it.'

He shakes a smile on to his face and flips open the lid, and there on the red bed inside is the strangest thing I ever did see. A metal S with six long hairs pulled along it with a black cup at the bottom. He don't wait for me to take it in or smell it or nothing, though. He picks it up and tucks it under his chin.

'This is my violin,' he says. 'An electric one. Do you want classic or contemporary?'

135

He picks up a thinner bar with more hair stretched along it and he places it over the S so the hairs are touching.

'Classic,' I say, not knowing what it means.

I have all these questions and I want to ask every single one, but then he moves his hand and this sound comes out that stops me right dead.

He moves his hand again, and the violin speaks something different. Then again and again, like he's stroking it, and the bar is singing away all happy, and the sound fills me right up.

Willow closes his eyes and he sways in time with his hand.

I can't think. I can't even breathe.

His music lifts me right up into the air and takes me over forests and seas. Strokes me from the top of my head right down to my toes. And I feel like I'm swimming in dry water and sinking into it deep, deep. And I ain't never wanting it to stop.

It does, though, finally.

The silence bites me awful hard and I feel like I've been running fast, I'm panting so hard.

He opens his eyes. 'Ele! Why are you crying?' He leans forward and touches my shoulder.

I ain't crying.

'Music,' he says, and he smiles at me all big.

I dry my eyes on my wrist.

'It's nice, huh?'

How to be an Outside Person – number eleven: Make music.

I think about my words for a long time. I think it in Other, and then I think it in People words, and then I say it out loud. 'Beautiful.'

And I din think it was gonna be possible, but that boy smiles even wider than before.

THIRTY-ONE

That music has churned something up inside me like butter in a barrel, and all that stuff I've been doing a mighty fine job of keeping a lid on until now goes and comes spilling out all at once.

I dream of Him. His whistle as he came towards the door. His whispers in my ear. The sounds He made when He'd fall asleep next to me, like there was a Bear living in His throat.

But then I dream of other things, too. Of Zeb singing to me when the sun bars went out. There were words, weren't there?

> *When you wish upon a star*
> *Makes no difference where you are*

I remember.

And I remember red lips singing those words, too. A shaking, lady's voice. Hands over my eyes so all I saw were stars. And wishes. Wishes that He would leave us alone tonight. That He wouldn't find us hiding.

Who is she, this lady?

And I remember telling Cow that singing was the sound a cooking pot made. And in my dream I'm back in the Tower, telling him all wide-eyed that I was wrong. That singing is the sound of wishes coming true.

When I wake up, I'm almost sad to see that I'm in Willow's room, not in the Tower with Cow's mad attempts to make himself a song. But then I remember that this is my wish, ain't it? Me being Outside is my wish come true.

And I ain't supposed to be thinking of the Inside.

Willow sat with me 'til I fell asleep last night, telling me all the names of things. I learnt words like 'spoon', and that the sun bars here are all called 'lights' – not only when they're above doors. The box in the corner is called a 'wardrobe', which is where Willow keeps all his 'clothes' in 'drawers'.

How to be an Outside Person – number two: Wear ~~extra-skins~~ clothes.

And the pictures on the wall of men wearing dark clothes and women wearing not much at all, those are called 'posters'. He took the ones with the women on them down when he saw me looking, his cheeks all red. And he din bring them back before he went off to school, which is where he said he learns stuff.

I want to learn everything.

I lift myself out of bed slowly, letting my body get used to being upright again, and walk over to the other door that Willow said leads to the 'bathroom' and it is a room that smells awful strong – something bright blue that gets right in the back of my throat. I din really notice much when he showed me the 'toilet' before, but now I'm better, I see that there's a whole lot of green in here. A green bowl with metal taps sticking out at one end that looks big enough to fit a whole person inside. And there's a smaller one beside it that I reckon would fit a Little Pig in just about right. And above it is what looks like a box with a whole other room hiding behind it.

I step forward, trying to close my nose from the smell of the place. And, as I do, I see a wild girl stepping towards me from out of the strange room, long yellow hair covering her face and body all the way down to –

I jump back.

So does the girl.

Only she ain't no girl, is she? She's *me*. And, if she's me, then I must have found myself a magic mirror, ready to tell me I'm the fairest in the land.

I'm feeling funny again, so I grip the edge of the small bowl with the taps and I take a step towards myself, as clear as if I'm somewhere else.

There I am, all scraggly and dirty under my hair. I ain't never seen me so clear before, 'cept in puddles on the floor. In the mirror, I look mighty ugly. Mighty, mighty. I can see my small nose clear as it is on my face, and my lips, too. And my hair is all wild and long like some kind of animal.

That mirror ain't telling me that I'm the fairest in the land.

I turn away and leave the bathroom.

Willow has all kinds of interesting stuff in his room for me to look at, anyway. He has a black book he called a 'laptop' that's got all the letters there are written on it. He's got other books, too – books called *J. S. Bach Konzert* and *Grade 7 Concert Pieces*, which have black blob writing in them that don't make no sense. I flick through a couple of them, my head thumping at the touch of pages in my fingers again.

I thought there might be more books on the Outside, ones with stories in that can help me make sense of everything, like the ones I had Inside. Then finally I find one with real words in.

The Life and Times of Wolfgang Amadeus Mozart.

Mozart. The person Willow said he'd go visit on his adventures with Angus. I pull out the book, all dusty, from its hiding place under all those others, and run with it to the bed to read it.

My fingers are shaking as they poke at the corners. There are more pages in this book than any of the ones back in the Tower – not that I'm thinking of them. On the front is a picture of a person I guess is Mozart. His grey hair's all rolled up like soggy paper, but he's smiling anyway, looking pleased as Pigs in his smart red clothes.

I open the book. And I read.

It ain't a book about no Ogres and Giants, but it's good anyway. It starts with a little boy who makes all the Kings and Queens of the land happy by playing with something called a 'piano'. He visits lands called 'Munich' and 'Vienna' and 'Prague'. There ain't no talk of Willow and Angus, but there's lots of 'concerts' where lots of important people come to watch him play.

I din realize playing could be so important.

I read with my nose almost touching the pages. The book smells different from the ones I know. It smells older somehow, and I can almost smell Willow on the pages, even though I can't see his name nowhere.

There's lots of talk of music in the book. So much that the words are almost singing off the page so I can hear them, long and sad, like Willow's violin.

Maybe it just feels sad 'cause of the ending. Mozart gets sick, just like I am. Instead of getting better, though, he dies. By the time I've finished reading, all the pages are wet.

Zeb's hands are reaching out towards me. His blue eyes are wide.

I close my eyes and hug the book tight to my chest. Then I put it under the pillow.

How to be an Outside Person – number twelve: Read all the books.

There ain't no more books in Willow's room. I tip out all the clothes from his wardrobe and open all the drawers I can find, but I don't find nothing but underpants.

I'll find more, though – more truths.

I do find something else when I'm looking. It flashes on when I clear away some of the junk on top of the table near the bed. It shows me all these pictures, like a magic mirror. Most are of a lady I guess to be Willow's Ashley-Mum, as the little 'un she's swinging above her head looks an awful lot like Willow around the eyes. Whoever she is, she's pretty. She has darker skin than even Willow, with big, wide eyes and hair all knotted into ropes, like someone has drawn it on. Something about her mouth makes me smile, even when she ain't smiling in the pictures herself. Her lips are always pouted like they're hiding stories. I'd like to have listened to them stories.

I also found a window hiding behind the flat white bars that Willow called the 'blinds'. I pulled them apart, stared out at the Outside and just about fell over at first. Turns out that I'm up high – higher than any tree I ever imagined – and I can see the grey world below, and it makes me feel weird and amazing at the same time.

Now I know how Rapunzel felt in her Tower with the window.

I saw my shed from above, the roof like a black drain. And I saw the walls, and I even saw other sheds and other walls way beyond that, and other houses and . . . and other windows like this. No one was looking back at me through them, but I felt like I might climb up on to any one of them roofs at any minute and go explore. 'Cause the world is big. Big and bigger than I ever thought.

I'm going to explore it. And I'm going to find me some books when I do.

I walk across to the bedroom door and my hand only hovers just a tiny bit before I swing it on open.

Ezra-Dad is already standing there, hand on his face like he's been wondering what to do about coming in, and when he sees me his forehead wrinkles up.

'I'm gonna go Outside,' I say, all breath.

'Aye.' He moves aside, so I can see some of the long room that's on the other side of the door. 'Ye'll want tae go downstairs, then.'

I nod, even though I ain't knowing what 'stairs' are to go down. He turns himself round and I follow, looking all what way inside the new room, big and high and yellow, with lots of doors going off into other rooms that I can't see –

'Whoa!'

My foot slips as the soft floor under my toes disappears. I look down, and the floor is suddenly miles below. My stomach is doing some falling of its own. I shout something like an 'oh'.

Then hands are on my arm, hands holding me up, letting me get my feet on to the floor and my back against the wall. Hands as big as beds and rough as wall.

I'm shaking all over. I look up at Ezra-Dad and see he's looking pale and surprised.

'Ye OK?'

His hands are out, like he's worried I might go and fall again. I want to prove that I'm fine, but my legs are feeling weird, so I slide down the wall 'til I'm sitting and can't see where the floor dips away.

'Didnae see the stairs, heh?'

I shake my head, my chest feeling all tight.

Ezra-Dad shuffles from foot to foot.

There's a bang, then a wallop of wind blows up to me from below the floor. There's a thump, then some more, then a rustle and a sniff. Then Willow appears, and when he sees me sitting his forehead rolls up like Ezra-Dad's.

Ezra-Dad wipes his hands down his trousers.

'Hey!' Willow says, sitting down right in the spot where I almost fell to my death. 'Er –' he darts a look at Ezra-Dad –

'what's going on?'

I swallow and don't say nothing. Nor does Ezra-Dad.

Willow raises an eyebrow. 'You want to come downstairs?'

I shake and nod my head at the same time so it comes out as a circle.

Willow looks at Ezra-Dad again, who coughs. 'She just . . . nearly fell.'

Willow's eyes are wide at me. 'You OK?'

I nod for true this time and look at Ezra-Dad, who saved me like a Woodcutter from a Wolf. He's looking up at the ceiling.

Willow creeps forward. 'Want to try coming down with me?'

I stretch my neck and try to look down the stairs, but Willow is in the way.

'We'll do it together. Kiddie-style, eh?'

I shuffle towards the hole with Willow, who sits on the top like it ain't nothing. I watch him use his hands and feet to slide his ass down bit by bit, kind of like how the Others used to shuffle themselves around the Tower.

This ain't the time to think on them, Ele.

I try the stair shuffle. Then we do it together. It takes an awful long time, as there are as many stairs as I have teeth, but when I get to the bottom Willow helps me up with a hand under the arm and I'm feeling mighty pleased.

How to be an Outside Person – number thirteen: Go downstairs.

The stairs lead to a long white room with four more doors.

Four.

'Who's in all of these?' I ask Willow, my hand still gripping hold of the bar on the side of the stairs. All the doors are closed.

Willow shrugs, pulling me forward. 'No one. It's just me and Dad here.'

The door in front of the stairs is different to the others. It has a mouth in it that's breathing the air of the Outside. We don't go through that one. Instead, I follow Willow as he pushes the door to the left open.

'This is the living room.'

And it is. It's beating red like the inside of a heart, with white shapes that look half chair and half bed, as well as a black square hanging on the wall over a hole housing a pile of sticks, like a Big Bad Wolf has blown something down in there.

'This is your room, too?' I say, my mouth all dry from being open so much.

'Aye,' Willow says. 'And there's more.'

More. And then I realize. Of course there'd be more rooms than in the Three Bears' house and the gingerbread house. Willow is a Prince, so this must be a real-life castle.

Willow pulls me out of the 'living room' and round the side of the stairs to a little door under them. Ezra-Dad tuts behind me. I peer in and see all sorts of things I now know to be shoes, all smelling a smell that zaps the top of my nose.

'This is the shoe cupboard,' he says. He smiles at the O of my mouth and shuts the door, shooting Ezra-Dad an *I told you so* smile.

'And this is the kitchen,' he says.

When he opens the door, all I see at first is light. Then I see tables and chairs. Then food – more food than I could ever want. Then windows, promising more Outside than I might ever need. I see that shed of mine sitting Outside, and I see what Willow must have been seeing, thinking of me in there and him out here.

And I watch him go towards another door in this room. A fifth door. *Five* doors. This one has light leaking in from the Outside. He's gonna open it. He's gonna open it and take me Outside.

And suddenly I ain't as ready to go as I thought I was.

THIRTY-TWO

I'm still in the kitchen when the sun has gone way down and Ezra-Dad has taken himself up to bed. Only Willow is left with me, hands propping up his chin and eyes rolling back into his head.

'Show me again.'

''sake, Ele. We've been over it a million times.'

But he slides off the chair and wanders over to me, bouncing round the 'kitchen worktop'. He turns on the tap. It's shiny and bent over a big bowl. A 'sink'.

How to be an Outside Person – number seven: Know all the Outside words.

I'm learning so many Outside words.

'Where does the water come from?'

He yawns. 'Some plant somewhere.'

'Plant like a tree?'

'Aye. Nae.' He groans. 'Who asks this stuff?'

He fills a big white box with water, sets it down, then it slowly starts to crackle. It's called a 'kettle'.

I open up a door to a box where the cups are kept. It's called a 'cupboard' or a 'press'. It squeaks something awful when it's opened, so I do it. A lot.

Willow groans again.

The 'tea' is kept in the box labelled TEA. Tea is little black dust in a round bag. You put it in the cup.

Willow sits back down again and rests his forehead on the table. I open the cold cupboard I now know to be a 'fridge', and a light comes on inside automatically, showing me three shelves and a see-through drawer. Inside the drawer are red and green balls called 'peppers', brown spotted balls called 'potatoes' – once Willow also called them 'tatties' – and a lighter brown ball with tufty hair called an 'onion', which made my eyes water when I licked it. The thing I want is hidden in the back of the fridge door, and it's in a tall cup called a 'bottle' and is as white as paper. It's called 'milk'. I recognize that word from the Cow in 'Jack and the Beanstalk', but I ain't never seen it in real.

I pour it out into the cups with the tea and hot water.

The teabags are taken out and the cups are stirred with a spoon, though we don't drink it from there. You have to wait until it's cooled down and then drink it from the cup. We go and sit at the table to wait for it.

How to be an Outside Person – number fourteen: Make tea.

This is our fifth cup. I wasn't sure about tea at first, but now it's my favourite.

Sitting at the table with Willow is Three Bears short of a scene in a book. I sit myself down and try not to wriggle about as much as my back and legs want to. Instead, I watch the clouds coming from the tea do a little dance up and around.

Willow rests his head in his hands again and looks at me. 'I can't believe you've not made tea before.'

'I have!'

'I meant before today.'

'Where are all the other Outside People?' I ask quick.

'Around here?' he says, blinking away his other thoughts. 'Erm, well, this is Scotland. Everyone is really spread out.'

Scotland. Willow's Kingdom must be mighty big if it's so spread out that you can't even see no Dragons in the sky. That'll explain why I ain't seen nothing yet, though. They're all hiding themselves away on other pages, waiting for me to go Outside and hunt them out.

I edge myself a little further away from the door.

That tired look is back in Willow's eyes again. He pokes at a hole in the table between us. 'There's just us here, really. And a few weirdos.'

I blow over the top of my tea and wish I was sitting on the floor.

Willow rubs his eyes. 'Things never used to be this quiet, though. When Mum was alive, there would always be sound somewhere. Singing. Music. Her cello. She was the one who got me into the violin, you know?' He glances up at me and smiles slightly. 'She said she needed a tenor to her bass. I wasn't any good, really – not then. But it was nice, playing with her. I dunno . . .' He rests his head back on his hand and his smile dribbles away between his fingers. 'It all sounds a bit empty now.'

And I know that. I knew it when Zeb went. All the Tower was filled with my own bad thoughts. There weren't no smiles from Zeb to lift them off the floor, nor words to keep me running. If I din have those Others . . .

I clear my throat. 'You got Ezra-Dad, though.'

Willow frowns. 'Nae, I don't. He doesn't care about anyone but himself. You know we can go for days sometimes without even saying a word to each other?'

'You don't always need words, though,' I say, squeezing the handle of my cup real tight.

Willow sighs, sitting back and rubbing his face in his hands. 'Aye, you do.' He looks at me out of the corner of his eye. 'What about your parents? Are they big talkers?'

Parents? My belly jumps up like the lights have just come on. What are parents, anyway? In the books, fathers are people who leave you alone in the woods, and mothers send Huntsmen to cut out your heart if you're too pretty.

I shrug.

Willow looks at me hard. 'You can tell me, you know. Where you're from. How you got here.'

I try taking a sip of my tea, but it's too hot and burns my lips. I wince.

Willow shifts from side to side, drumming his fingers on the table. 'Ele?'

I disappear under my hair.

'Your accent –'

'I ain't lying!' I shout, banging my hands on the table and making Willow jump. 'I'm from here, like I said, OK?'

Willow blinks, his hands up. 'OK, sorry for asking.' He frowns. 'But, you know, you should tell us. If there's anyone looking for you, we should know.'

'There ain't no one looking for me.' I keep myself bent forward, all the words I ain't saying eating at my belly. The Others. Jack. All trapped Inside. Are they thinking of me?

And Him. What about Him?

How to be an Outside Person – number five: Don't think about the Inside.

Willow nods at me, but he knows. He can see my Inside on me like I have it written all over my skin.

'Come on. It's late.'

He stands up noisily and I follow, putting the cups in the sink like he showed me. He stomps up the stairs on his feet like it ain't nothing, and I follow him up with my eyes 'til he disappears. I try putting my foot on the bottom step and lifting myself up. It hurts my legs in strange places.

I'm awful wobbly, so I sit down and try sliding myself up. But it ain't the same without Willow here.

It don't feel right to be up there tonight, anyway. Not with his words ringing in my ears.

I go into the kitchen again, and curl up on the shiny floor, instead.

Even with the lights off, it's mighty bright in here. There's yellow light coming from Outside someplace and it's making me think of suns. I lie awake on my back, staring at a long crack in the ceiling, stretching from the door to the dark light bulb.

I got to be better at being Outside. Even making tea and speaking all the words ain't enough. Willow knows something. And I know it's only a matter of time 'til he goes and finds out about that Inside.

And then what?

THIRTY-THREE

Willow comes down in the morning and finds me sitting in front of the door opposite the stairs, looking out through the rectangle hole in the middle of it. I got my hands poked through it and my nose buried deep in the Outside air, so I don't hear him come down the stairs and up behind me.

'Have you been here all night?'

I jump and trap my fingers in the flap, cussing. I shake my head, sucking on my red knuckles.

He raises his eyebrow, but I ain't lying. I've been in the kitchen, trying to make myself come over to this door.

'You can go out, you know. It's not locked.'

He leans over me, presses down the door handle and pulls it towards us. All the Outside comes rushing in at me all at once.

How to be an Outside Person – number four: Go Outside.

I push the door shut again.

'That's OK!' I shout, my heart hammering. 'I don't need to go Outside. I'm fine looking through the hole.'

Willow looks at me funny before smiling and helping me up. 'Sure you are. I ran you a bath, actually, if you want it? I . . .' He looks down at the hole in his sock. 'I guess it's to say sorry for barraging you with questions last night.' He shakes his head. 'I hate that.'

I nod, trying not to look at him. I don't want him thinking no more on last night.

He leads me up the stairs, and I make it mainly on my feet this time, with him helping me. I'm wondering what a 'bath' is.

He gives me a big orange blanket that feels like carpet, which is the soft thing on all the floors in here, and I follow him into the bathroom. I look into the large bowl in the corner and see a waterfall splashing up white and making clouds that settle on top of the water.

Willow smiles at me, turning off the tap and stopping the waterfall. The white still stays though, in big bubbles that are steaming up and making the air all warm and wet.

'I'll be just outside – I have some free periods this morning. Enjoy your bath.'

Bath.

He hangs my blanket off the thing I know to be a toilet and leaves the door open a crack behind him.

I don't waste no time taking my clothes off and getting in that water – although I need to do it awful slow, as it burns my feet at first, making it feel like I'm on fire. When I'm finally sitting in it, though, I feel like I'm back in the Outside Inside my Head, with all the green, and white water. I can almost smell me those trees and hear that wind running right through them.

It feels like nothing I've ever felt before, hot water. It's like sitting in a cup of tea all to myself. I take a strange-smelling thing that I think to be 'soap' – like the one in *The Alphabet Book* – off the side of the bath and I rub it all over me. It makes these bubbles that take my smell right off me and make me feel about as clean as I ever felt.

I splat my hands in the bubbles.

Are you forgetting us, Ele?

All the clouds of heat in the air make the whole bathroom slip to the right, and I put my hands out to steady myself, blinking.

'Jack?' I say, my voice all echoey. I look about me, but don't see nothing. 'Is that you?'

Nothing.

I swear I heard him, though. Like he was in this room with me someplace.

I frown and blink some more. It's awful hot. I got black spots in my eyes now, and all the air is being sucked out from the heat.

I shake my head. 'I ain't supposed to be thinking of you now.'

The bathroom slips again, and all of a sudden they're all I can see. Eyes in the dark, looking at me. Waiting for me to come back in through the door.

My breath is coming out in strange little gasps. I reach out blindly and pull myself out of the water and find the air over near the sink. The Outside starts coming back in patches. I wipe my hand over the magic mirror, and watch myself coming out between the lines of my fingers. The blue in my eyes has almost all been sucked down the big black drain in the middle of them.

'I can't go back,' I whisper to myself. 'I'm Outside.'

But the girl in that mirror don't look Outside. She's still got Jack's wall knuckles on her hands, His bruises on her arms. She can still feel Bee's fingers brushing through her hair.

It's all giving her away.

How to be an Outside Person – number three: Look like them.

I rummage around in the bathroom for something sharp and find it on two little spikes joined in the middle, with holes just the perfect size for my fingers at each end. I hold them up to my head and I watch myself get lighter in the mirror as I hack off all the bits of Inside me.

Jack's knocks.

The Others' games.

Zeb's wide, sad eyes.

Gone.

I stand in a big pile of yellow, and I see my face all clear and bright white. My eyes are already showing those trees inside of them.

THIRTY-FOUR

Willow must hear me coming out of the bathroom, as he comes running up the stairs two at a time soon as I do.

'How was – whoa!'

His eyes brush over my hair – or what's left of it, anyway – wide as I ever saw them.

And I wanna roll my eyes and make it into no big deal, but I can feel myself heating up under his looking. I stare at my feet.

'What shampoo did you use?'

He's laughing nervously, but me not knowing what 'shampoo' is, I keep quiet, wishing he weren't blocking my way to hiding back in bed.

He looks over my shoulder. 'Did you cut it all with the nail scissors?'

He gets closer and I move my head away, shrugging.

'Hey,' he says, moving his face into my line of sight and getting so close I can smell the Outside on his breath. 'It looks nice. Really.'

He smiles, and – goddammit – I do, too.

'It needs tidying up a bit, though. Those scissors weren't really made for Rapunzel.'

And I laugh that time, 'cause I know exactly what he means.

'Stay there.' He runs back down the stairs and I dive back into the bathroom, looking myself over in the mirror before he sees. He's right – it's pretty untidy, as it goes. Especially when you look at the neat little line of his hair.

But it's gone. Ain't no ladder for no Witch to be climbing up into my head no more.

He comes in, catching me smiling at myself, but he don't say nothing. If anything, that boy looks mighty scared. He's holding these big blades, as big as my own hand.

I raise my eyebrow.

'I'm not going to stab you, Ele. I just don't know how to cut hair.'

This time I do roll my eyes. 'Me neither, and I managed just fine.'

He laughs. 'Face the mirror.'

I look back at myself and he comes to stand right behind me, clear as day over my head, on account of him being so tall. He makes my skin look whiter than white, but it's kind of nice to see my face alongside his.

We're different in all kinds of ways. But we're the same now, too.

He lets out a big breath of air and meets my eyes in the mirror.

'So . . . how would you like it?'

'Like yours.'

He starts laughing again and don't even stop when I give him a look.

'I'm not sure my hair would suit you, Ele. Let's go with something a bit more feminine.'

I shrug. His hands feel cold on my skin, which is still hot from the bath. He's only meant to be tidying up all the jagged bits, but he's being mighty slow about it, trimming only tiny bits at a time. Halfway through, my legs get awful tired, so he brings in a chair for me to sit on, though I'm not so good at that without fidgeting. We end up on the floor – me sitting in the way my legs know how, and him crawling around any what way to see me from all the angles he can.

'There. Oh no – wait.' He trims a bit more above my right ear and I hear the snip like a whisper. 'OK. There.'

He stands up. Then, thinking about it, he helps me up too, looking worried.

I turn to the mirror and, well, would you look at that? He's done a mighty fine job. I lean in for a closer look and see that the lines round my neck and ears are all straight-cut like his now, though I've still got my mess of hair on the top, with a few bits floating down near my eyes. You might even say I look nice.

But, most importantly, you might say I look like I'm an Outside Person.

'You want to keep any of this?' Willow says, holding up bits of yellow hair as long as his arm.

I keep my eyes on my eyes. 'No,' I say. 'That ain't mine no more.'

THIRTY-FIVE

I couldn't be more like an Outside Person.

I have dinner with Willow and Ezra-Dad, sitting at their table in the kitchen and eating food that's as hot as a bath. It makes me think of eating something real and still beating, and, I got to say, I don't like it much.

I eat it anyway, trying not to spit it all back out again, as Willow told me it's 'rude' when I did that the first time, meaning that it hurts their feelings somehow. It's not like I'm spitting it all over them, but I decide to keep quiet on the matter.

How to be an Outside Person – number fifteen: Don't spit no food out.

One nice thing about eating all together, though, is that Willow gets to put on some music that comes out of a little black box on the table to the side of the kitchen door. I spent a good amount of time looking for the people making the sounds, but Willow says it's just a 'recording'.

Here's what else I've learnt about eating at the table: it happens three times a day. And it turns out that you got to eat different stuff according to where the sun is in the sky. In the morning, Willow heats us up some porridge, which I remember well from 'Goldilocks and the Three Bears'. If Ezra-Dad was ever anything, it was a big orange Bear. And I guess that makes me a baby Bear, 'cause I like everything just right – not full of the stuff Willow calls 'sugar', which makes my throat tickle.

In the afternoon, we eat something that's kind of like thick water, which Willow calls 'soup'. It tastes all right, even if it is the strangest colour you ever did see in a food.

Dinner is my favourite, though, 'cause of the music.

How to be an Outside Person – number sixteen: Eat at the table.

'Did you enjoy that, Ele?' Willow says with his eyebrow raised when I'm licking the plate clean.

I shrug. 'It's all right.'

Ezra-Dad starts laughing under that 'beard' of his. He does it with his mouth closed, like he shouldn't be making no sounds.

I smile.

Willow looks from me to Ezra-Dad, clearing his throat. 'I found my book under your pillow, Ele. You can have it, you know. If you want it.'

I drop my fork, turning in my seat to look him over for lies. 'You mean I can keep it? All for myself?'

'If yer looking for books,' Ezra-Dad says, 'ah got one ye can have, if ye want it.'

I spin back to him. 'Yes!'

Willow frowns at him. 'Since when do you read?'

Ezra-Dad shrugs. 'Since when dae ye?'

Willow's cheeks go as red as Ezra-Dad's hair. 'Come on, Ele. I've got something to show you, anyway.'

I follow him out of the kitchen, beaming at Ezra-Dad, who gives me what he'd call a 'wee smile'.

Willow pushes me through the door to the living room and on to one of those big chairs that look as comfy as beds. They bounce me up and down when I land in them. The white is made of something slippery, though, and I have to sit myself up properly to stop from sliding right on to the floor.

Willow sits down next to me and throws the Mozart book on to my lap.

Mine?

I daren't touch it. I ain't never had nothing that was all mine, not really. Course, I liked to think my space in the Tower was mine, and Jack was mine, and the Outside Inside my Head was mine. But I ain't had nothing I could touch that was just mine before.

I stop my thoughts, shaking my head.

How to be an Outside Person – number seventeen: Have things that are only yours.

I stroke the corners of the book. 'Thank you.'

Willow smiles. 'I wanted to show you ... We've got another book somewhere. It's, well, it's kind of special. You want to see it?'

I'm feeling dizzy with all the nodding I'm doing.

Willow jumps up and over to a white ladder on the wall with all kinds of junk piled up in its holes.

'I know it's here somewhere,' he mutters, moving a pile of loose pages and looking underneath.

I stare down at the book. *My* book. All about music and places. About the adventures Willow used to have with Angus. It's like this book is a little piece of Willow – all mine.

I hold it tight.

'Here it is!' Willow calls, pulling something small from under a box of circles. He blows on the top, smiling at the cover before bringing it over to me.

'This was my mum's favourite. I think it's pretty old, so be careful.'

I hold it very carefully, my hands shaking. I can smell that it's old – something kind of like the cupboard under the stairs with all those old shoes mixed with that paper smell I know like it's my own. I lift the book to my nose and breathe it all in.

The cover is hard and covered in dirt. Even so, the picture of the golden girl on the front shines out at me like it's made of sun.

'She looks like me,' I whisper, tracing my finger round the circle she's in.

Willow leans over. 'Huh. I guess she does a bit, eh? Before the haircut, mind you.' He flicks one of the short curls on my head and I smooth it back down. 'Open it up, then.'

The first page is torn at the side and someone has written *When you can't look on the bright side, I will sit with you in the dark – 1904* in blue at the top. Maybe they din realize there were already words inside.

Alice's Adventures in Wonderland it says next to a drawing that's lost all its colour. My hands are shaking like crazy now, wanting to pull apart all the pages and read every word.

'Have you read it before?' Willow asks. 'It's a bit different from the film.'

I shake my head, opening up the next pages, where more and more pictures are waiting, all with the girl in them.

'I think my mum liked it 'cause it's about coming to a different place and everything being different. Kind of like what it's like for you, I guess.'

I pull my eyes away from the book to look at him, my insides wriggling like fingers pulling on bones. 'She came from somewhere else?'

Willow nods. 'Aye, she was born in Jamaica. Moved to Scotland when she was five or something, I think.' He smiles. 'We're all mad here.'

I let out a big breath, nodding as I fall back in the chair. 'Thank you,' I say again.

I don't know what he says back. I don't notice when he leaves, or see if it was him that put that cold cup of tea next to the chair. By the time I've finished reading all the words and seeing every line of every picture, though, he's gone. And I'm left with one line in the book floating around beside me like Ashley-Mum has painted it in the air, like what Willow said she used to do with trees.

It's no use going back to yesterday, because I was a different person then.

I've fallen down a rabbit hole and there ain't no going back out of it. There might be food that will turn me big and small, and Queens that want my head, and I might not know how to play croquet with a flamingo, but that's all right. 'Cause it's normal to be seeing stuff for the first time. It don't mean that I ain't no Outside Person just 'cause I ain't never seen a cat disappear before.

And, if Ashley-Mum could see all of this stuff new and still make Willow smile in the way he does when he talks about her, then I guess it's OK for him to know that I ain't from here.

He don't need to know all about that Inside, though. I was a different person then.

Today I'm an Outside Person.

THIRTY-SIX

I din sleep much last night. I lay on my bed listening to all the sounds the house was making and wondering how anyone could sleep in such a racket. The walls were knocking when there weren't nothing on the other side. The windows were snoring. The lamp by the side of my bed was humming.

Everything was alive and waiting for me to get up and go discover it. And I kept thinking of Alice and Mozart in the books. How they went out and had their adventures like it weren't nothing. So I made myself a deal right there and then: I'm gonna go Outside. Soon as Willow wakes up and can take me.

I wait until I can hear noises downstairs before plodding slowly down, even though I want to run down like Willow does. I don't find him in the living room, nor in the shoe cupboard under the stairs. I run into the kitchen and don't find him there neither. Just Ezra-Dad sitting at the table on his own.

'Where's Willow?'

'He's at school.'

'Already?'

He glances up at a circle with numbers on it. 'Aye.'

'Oh.'

He looks back down at the white on the table that looks like some kind of big book with floppy pages, and I almost stop thinking of the Outside right there and then to read it with him. I can't, though. I've got to do it.

Today, my heart thumps out. *Today*.

I walk over to the back door. It's all window apart from a stripe of brown across the middle of it, but you can't see nothing out of it 'cept light. The window is all scratched up, like something big has been ripping at it to get in, lines all criss-crossing and clouding it up.

Maybe it was a Dragon.

I look at the door.

How to be an Outside Person – number four: Go Outside.

'Key's in the drawer,' Ezra-Dad says, pointing at a side table that I ain't never noticed before.

There's all sorts of stuff inside the drawer: matted white hair, bits of metal, small boxes that say MATCHES, PLAYING CARDS and PLASTERS, all torn up and falling apart. I move some of it about, enjoying how it all feels in my hands, then I see it.

The key.

It's a gold metal bar with teeth on the end, just like the key from *The Alphabet Book*.

I scramble over to the back door, tap the key on the side of it and push.

Nothing.

I try again, the metal key clinking on the metal door frame as they hit each other.

Still it don't open.

My hands start shaking.

'Let me,' Ezra-Dad says, suddenly behind me. He takes the key out of my hands and pushes it into the hole under the door handle. He twists the key and the door cusses at him. Then he pushes the handle down and pulls the door open.

The back garden.

Ezra-Dad stands there, hand on the door to stop it swinging closed, looking at me looking out.

It's grey. It's cold. It blows.

'Go on then,' he says.

I don't move.

He starts shuffling, looking at my feet. 'Ye want a piggyback or something?'

I look at him.

He shrugs. 'Ye havnae any shoes, so ah thought maybe . . .'

I nod.

'Well, OK then.'

He turns round and opens his arms out, looking like he wants me to climb on to his back. I take a step towards him, unsure I've got it right, as he's not no steed, but he don't say I'm wrong as I jump up and wrap my legs round his middle. He catches me under the knees and then lifts me up.

Then he steps Outside. With me.

I'm *Outside*.

All the air blows at the back of my neck, inspecting my new haircut. I hold my head up high and show it off to the sun.

The sun is hiding behind a cloud. It must feel awful stupid for hurting me before, now that it sees I'm a real-life Outside Person who goes Outside.

Ezra-Dad starts moving bumpily and I hold him tighter, his beard scratching at my arms.

He coughs, and I feel the lump in his throat on my arms. I move them.

'Sorry,' I say.

He grunts. 'Where tae?'

I grip him tight. The air is tickling at my toes. The floor seems an awful long way down. I keep watch for Dragons.

I point to the shed. 'There.'

Ezra-Dad stops and bends down, picking up my sword that I dropped all that time ago. He throws it back into the shed. Inside is all the same stuff there was before, all shapes and things clumped together. Ezra-Dad tuts, muttering about it being Willow's job to clean it up.

I think back to when I first opened my eyes to find I was Outside, looking at all the stuff and not knowing what nothing was. Now I know those extra-skins are clothes, and what's holding them are bin bags. The boxes at the back are wardrobes, drawers, chests. My sword – that's just a broom. And my shield is the lid of a bin. And the picture of the trees still propped up in my corner – that's a painting.

Ezra-Dad drops my legs and his breath at the same time, holding on to the door frame like he's worried he's gonna fall over. I hop round the side of him, rubbing my feet where I landed. He don't see me. All he sees is that painting, like he ain't never seen no trees before neither.

We look at it together.

'Birch,' I say, pointing. 'Pine. Willow. Ash –'

I don't get to finish, though. He leaves suddenly, the door to the shed swinging back, so I have to run to catch it before it shuts.

I don't want to be trapped Inside all over again.

'Wait!' I say, as he marches towards the back door.

For a second, I think he's gonna keep walking away. But he stops. Sees me, his hands in his beard. He walks over and bends down, so I can climb up on to his back.

He takes me down the path and into the kitchen and I'm careful not to accidentally strangle him again. I wait for him as he locks the door and puts the key back in the drawer.

And then, just to prove I couldn't be more of an Outside Person, I make him tea.

He don't say nothing, but he does sit down, hands halfway over the tabletop, like he's reaching on out to me. I make the tea the best I ever made it. I even do the hot part. I put it down in front of him and look at his hands, all scratched up like he's been banging them on walls all his life, nails so short they're looking like a new knuckle.

He's looking at me, too, expecting me to say things. So I ask him a question.

'The trees – where are they?'

Ezra-Dad takes a deep breath in and looks mighty tired all of a sudden. His eyes leave mine for the grey Outside again.

'They died with her.'

He sips his tea. I sip mine. His words have frozen up my insides, though, making the tea feel extra-hot in my chest. It hurts.

The trees died with her.

THIRTY-SEVEN

The trees are all dead.

I make it up the stairs and into bed without even thinking. I pull the covers over my head and, in the darkness, the bad thoughts come. They follow each other like drips from a tap, getting faster until you can't turn the tap off.

They mix up together until they paint me a real picture. A memory.

What happened after Zeb died.

Waiting by the door. Not sleeping. Not eating. Not thinking.

Until . . . footsteps.

And I ain't Outside no more. I'm Inside again.

I think about standing. Think about doing something when He comes through the door – maybe whacking Him on the head, or making a run for it. But I can't move, even if I want to. Zeb's tried every one of those things before.

He's too strong.

He's coming.

The footsteps stop on the other side of the door. There's a pause. Then green.

Whoosh! Air from Outside. And there He is, all big and shadow, looking into my empty corner. He spots me near the door, cusses loud and slams it closed real quick, then hurls His leg back and kicks it out again.

Thwack!

His foot hits me so hard it feels cold. Like that numb feeling you get when you dunk your head under the tap, but all at once. All in my chin bone.

And *smack!* I hit the floor, my neck swinging like a door and slamming the back of my head into it, too.

The air is full of broken metal. It's buzzing in my head and melting in my mouth.

Blood.

Hands on my arm, lifting me up. I can't see. Ain't even got no thoughts but exclamation marks. Then I'm upright and the floor is taking my jaw down and the pain kicks in.

I scream out. It hurts me something terrible, though, so I just gargle on my own blood, hands trying to keep my teeth from falling out.

'Just let me see, will yer!'

Him. His fingers push into my mouth. Pain bites me. I scream again.

'Goddamn it, girl! What yer doin' so close to the door, anyhow?'

He's cussing, hitting my hands away, moving my jaw this way and that. My eyes start working again. He looks worried.

I hate Him.

'Whrrrr,' I groan, still trying to hold my mouth together.

He stops poking. Eyes darken. 'What did yer . . . did yer just *say* somethin'?'

I don't speak to Him. Someone else does, using my throat. 'Whrrrrr!'

He blinks. My blood is streaked on His face.

'Yer tryin' to say "where"?'

I look at Him. At His grey eyes with dark pits. I throw my gaze over to the door and back at Him.

He rubs more of my blood across His chin. 'Yer looking for the boy?'

He laughs, and it's like He's still kicking me. Again. Again. The pain grows up inside of me like a tree, and I pull my fist back ready to smack Him in the face and –

He catches my hand. Sound is swallowed. His lip curls real evil.

'Yer boy is *gone*. Dead. You ever so much as think about doin' what he did, I'll kill yer an' all.'

He forces me back against the wall with His knee, leaning in, and pushes His finger into my chin.

Pain thumps around the bones in my head.

'But I won't be so quick about it with yer.'

He pushes His finger in some more and white-hot noise fills me up and, just when I reckon I can't take it no more, it stops.

He lifts Himself up, strides to the door. My hands are reaching on out, trying to claw Him back by the boots, but He's too fast. I'm crawling, knees scratching up on the floor. Door opens. I throw myself after Him.

I don't make it. It closes. The light switches to red.

Outside

And I take up my hands and I hit the door – hard. With all I have. The pain thwacks through me, but I need it. I need it somewhere other than my head and my jaw, so I do it again. And again. I do it until it's all I have and all I am and –

Bang.

I whack my hands on that window again and again, making a racket that goes right up the bones of my arms and screams inside my head. I see that Outside and I hate it. Hate it for being all grey and not green, and cold and not warm. For not having no Mermaids or gingerbread houses that I can see. For having a sun that hurts me and mirrors that lie to me.

For not having no trees.

I slap that glass 'til it starts turning red. The sky turns pink. Lines drip down. My hands scream out for me to stop, but I keep pounding, the sound filling up my chest, 'til I can't take no more and I start throwing myself at the glass instead. My whole body, then just my head. My stupid head that can't follow no rules. That keeps thinking of the Inside.

Bang.

Bang.

Things start to turn purple. I hear my name being called out.

Bang.

'Ele! Stop that!'

Bang.

And then hands. Hands rough as wall on my neck, on my face. I fight them off, trying to throw myself out again, 'cause now that I've stopped all the hurt has time to start spreading.

But they're too strong. I fall into those arms and they hold me real tight.

'It's OK.' His voice sounds awful loud with my ear to his chest. He smells of tables. 'It's OK.'

His hands are on my cheeks. They pull my head up, out of the dream, into the real.

Ezra-Dad. Brown eyes. Orange eyebrows.

My jaw ain't broke.

I hold on to his hands like they're holding me up. Look at him. He don't break his eye contact. Not to watch my blood rain down on the window. Not to ask me why I was doing it. Just to be there.

I grip him. My breath wheezes in and out of me.

'The trees,' I gasp. 'They're dead?'

Ezra-Dad's eyes turn sad, but they don't leave mine for one second. 'Nae,' he says. 'Ah shouldnae have said that. There are still trees.'

The air rushes back into my lungs. I swallow it down, spitting out the rest of my dream. I pull him towards me, wrapping my hands over his neck so he has to bend right over, and I hold him to me tight. My hands leave streaks of red on his shoulders.

He holds me back.

We stand like that. Together. Must be for days.

'It's OK,' he says.

And slowly, slowly, I start to believe him.

Something shuffles at the door behind me, and Ezra-Dad drops me like too-hot tea. I stumble round, blinking.

Willow stands at the door. He's got something all wrapped up in pink paper by his side. His mouth hangs open.

'Willow!' I rub my eyes, and Ezra-Dad is trying to hide his, too. When I finally look at him, I see that he's looking mighty strangely at Ezra-Dad. At the bloody handprints on his shoulders. At the tears in his beard.

I rub my hands down my dress. 'Ezra-Dad –'

Willow flicks his eyes to me. 'It's just Ezra, Ele. He's not your dad.'

I bite my stupid tongue. 'Yeah, I know –'

'Well, I don't know if you do.' He throws the pink package he was holding on to the bed. It rolls off on to the floor and all these different-coloured balls burst out.

'Will,' Ezra-Dad starts, but Willow steps back.

'Nae,' Willow says, more like a grunt than a word. 'You're OK.'

He don't meet my eye as he leaves.

I go to follow him, but Ezra-Dad catches my shoulder and pulls me back.

'Bed,' he grunts.

'I ain't tired,' I say, trying to shrug him off.

'Now.'

I scowl at him. He's got my blood all over him. Looking at it makes me feel funny. I get into bed.

'What did I do?' I ask, nodding to the door.

Ezra-Dad brings a green bag back from the bathroom and starts wiping my hands with a cloth that smells of bad things. It stings, but he does it gentle.

'Ignore him.'

I scowl again. 'I don't want to.'

The cloth comes away all red. He throws it away and wraps up my palms in white cloths from a pack that says BANDAGES on the front.

'He's just being childish.'

I ain't sure that's all it is.

Ezra-Dad finishes up with my hands, then wipes my blood off the window with another cloth and backs out of the room.

'OK?' he says, hovering in the door.

I nod slowly.

He leaves, and my ears follow him into the room that Willow is sleeping in.

'What?' Willow's voice is muffled through the wall.

'Ele,' Ezra-Dad says, 'she's nae from yer school, is she?'

My heart quickens.

'That's what you came in here to talk about?'

'Willow. Answer the question, will ye?'

I hear Willow sigh. 'Close the door.'

There is a squeak and a click and their voices turn to mumbles. I get out of bed and tiptoe over to the wall and press my ear to it.

I can't make out their words. Their weird way of saying things is difficult anyway, even without a wall in the way. They're talking about me, though. I know it.

The door opens again and I listen as Ezra-Dad leaves Willow's room. I expect him to come marching on back in here and tell me that I can't stay here no more. Or, worse, that I'll have to go back *there*.

I clench my fists at my sides.

But Ezra-Dad don't come for me. He sighs and treads downstairs, in that slow, careful way he has.

They ain't kicking me out yet, then. So what are they doing?

I walk to the end of the bed. The pink thing Willow flung is all bent and broken on the floor. I pick it up, sneezing.

It's paper, and it's open at the top. Inside, there are more of them coloured balls, some of them like open fists. They are all poking up out of green sticks tied up together with string. And I know what they are. I know from the picture of the cottage in the woods in 'Rapunzel'. They're flowers.

I don't breathe. My wrapped-up hands are all shaky as they poke at the little coloured fingers, soft as Bee's cheeks. I bend down and pick up all the broken ones on the floor, trying to fit them all back inside.

Flowers. For me. Real flowers.

I tuck myself back up in bed, resting the flowers next to my head. They smell mighty strong and itch at my eyes, but I don't stop looking at them. The big red ones all closed up. The wide, flat purple ones. The white ones huddled together like clouds. And my favourite of them all: the ones that look like leaves.

'Why did he throw you away?' I whisper to them. 'Why you and not me?'

Some loud music starts banging up a storm from the wall between my room and Willow's. It ain't like violin music. It's angrier. I listen with everything I can, but I can't make out the words.

Willow really needs to work on his knocking.

THIRTY-EIGHT

'What are ye doing?' Ezra-Dad asks me as he comes up the stairs, smelling of breakfast.

I'm sitting on the floor in front of Willow's door. I can hear him getting ready for school, cussing to himself.

'I want to say thank you,' I say. 'For the flowers.'

Ezra-Dad raises an eyebrow, but grunts, stepping on by me. 'I wouldnae talk tae him in the morning if ah was ye. He's a terror until noon.' He stops and turns round, his hand in his beard. 'Ah have something for ye, actually. If ye go downstairs . . .'

I jump to my feet. 'Is it a book?'

He mumbles, 'Might be, if ye want tae ruin the surprise . . .'

I fumble downstairs as quick as I can, my bandaged-up hands sliding down the banister. When I get to the living room, though, there ain't no book waiting for me. Just my other two, sitting on a shelf of their own that someone has gone and cleared for me. They're both stood up tall next to each other and beside them there's enough room for even more books. Maybe even *twelve* more, if they were little, like *The Alphabet Book*.

I hear Ezra-Dad behind me and, when I turn round, I see he's holding something that looks mighty like a book.

I snatch it from his hands.

It's all warm from where he's been holding it. It's huge. Bigger than any book I ever did see before. And on it are leaves.

The Gardener's Companion.

'Thank you,' I whisper.

I catch his eye looking at me, even though he grunts to cover it up.

The pages are shiny, like they've never been read before. It ain't a story – I can tell that from the very first page. It's just like *An Encyclopaedia of British Trees*, but this one is about all kinds of different plants. Flowers, like the ones Willow got me. Bushes of all different types. There ain't many words, but the pictures are everything. They're alive. In this book, they're alive.

'Now, I'm gonnae tell ye something, OK?' Ezra-Dad says, looking all about the room so I ain't sure he's even talking to me. 'Plants are . . . are a bit like folk.'

I flop down on the chair, looking for faces in the pictures of flowers. ''Cause they're all green?'

'Nae.'

''Cause they need watering all the time?'

'Aye, they do, but –'

''Cause –'

'Och! Just let me finish, will ye?'

I bite my lip and smile, still flicking through the pages.

'Plants are like people 'cause they need a lot tae grow, OK?' He starts pacing up and down, his hands in his pockets.

'Some of them shoot right up, even when yer nae paying any attention tae them. But others . . .' He eyes the ceiling, where Willow is stomping around, turning off his music. 'Others need a wee bit more time. Ye got tae give them more room tae grow.'

I run my finger down the edge of the pages and nod. 'OK.'

And, when Willow comes downstairs and heads out of the door, I don't try to meet him on the way. I give him his room to grow.

THIRTY-NINE

Ezra-Dad reads a book called the newspaper at the table. He gets a new one every day. I sit next to him and read all the bits with him.

'What does "for sale" mean?' I ask, stopping him from turning the page.

He grumbles, 'What it says.'

He moves my finger out of the way and he turns the page.

For a while, I think Ezra-Dad likes to read fast, but when I watch his eyes move I see he's mainly just reading one or two things – not all the words.

'Why ain't you reading that?' I ask, pointing to a big square that says: *You could be entitled to up to £5,000 in mis-sold PPI*. It even has a funny picture on it of a woman wearing ear-hats.

He grunts. 'Advert.'

'But it says you could get money.'

He licks his finger and uses it to turn the page again. 'Pack of lies.'

I sit back, shaking my head. 'Everyone knows books are filled with truth.'

'Aye, but this isnae a book.'

I don't like the newspaper much after that. Seems a bit stupid to me, reading things that ain't real. It don't make much sense, anyway. It starts off telling the story of a man who was caught having something called an 'affair' with a lady, and then next moment they're gone and we're hearing about something called the 'Olympic Games' and 'athletes'. And it ends with men called 'footballers', who I guess ball people's feet up. It ain't a nice ending.

It's nice reading with Ezra-Dad, though. When he's done with the newspaper, he tidies up the kitchen, which I do with him. He gets a cloth and wipes it over the table and the sink. I wipe a cloth over them, too, but I get my bandages all wet and need to take them off. He watches me out of the corner of his eye, but don't say nothing. He takes the bin bag out of the bin and ties it up. I grab a handle and haul it out, too. He throws clothes into a wide mouth called the washing machine. I throw some of my clothes in there, too, though he ups and runs out of the room when I take off my dress.

Ezra-Dad turns on the moving picture in the living room that he says is called a TV. We watch a programme about people called 'police'. They ask a lot of questions about something called a 'murder' and put the people who lie about it in cages. I ask Ezra-Dad to change the programme. He does.

Mainly, we watch stuff to do with making things. His favourite is a programme called *Scrapheap Challenge*, where people are in two groups and an excited man screams at them to make something up out of all the metal things in the

Outside shed. Ezra-Dad don't tell me it's his favourite, but he watches it all the way through without switching, so I know.

'That man shouts too much,' I say, eating the crisps out of Ezra-Dad's bowl.

He smiles. He don't think I see, but I do.

FORTY

Ezra-Dad is going Outside.

He said he's going to 'work'. I ain't sure what he means by that. When I asked him, he mumbled a lot about 'inheritance money' and 'being laid off', until he said that work was just something he did to fill his time – like reading, or watching TV.

I'm watching him get ready for work from the stairs. He's putting on his coat and shoes and a hat for his head, and I ain't got none of those.

He puts his hand on the door, thinking hard about opening it. I pull my knees up close, waiting for the air.

'Ye can come, if ye want.'

He says it to the door, so for a moment I ain't sure that he ain't talking to it. He turns to me eventually, though, and I poke my fingers in between my toes so I'm holding my own hands.

I rock forward and back. I bite my lip. 'Piggyback?'

Ezra-Dad shakes his head.

I put my head down again. 'Then no thank you.'

Still he don't leave. He keeps his hand on the door, rocking like me. Then he lets out a sigh. 'OK then.'

I stick my head up. 'You'll do it?'

He nods.

I jump up and put on the Outside things that he hands me: a yellow coat, all big and puffy, making me look as big as Cow – no, as big as a fridge – and a red scarf. I find shoes in the shoe cupboard that fit me and put them on.

Ezra-Dad watches me dress and waits for me to join him at the door.

'OK.'

He bends down, and I jump on his back like last time. And I'm like a Prince jumping on my steed, ready for adventure.

'Onwards!' I shout, pointing to the door.

He looks round at me, eyebrow raised, and I grin at him. He grunts back, just like a real horse.

He opens the door and we take my first steps Outside the front. My smile gets blown away by the wind and my heart starts beating up a storm. I hold on to Ezra-Dad's coat as tight as I can.

It's a brilliant white day and the sky is all frothy from jumping over cloud rocks. I can kind of feel where the sun is, though, high in the sky and making a bright hole. All the light shines on the grey floor and walls and makes them look glittery, like metal.

It's still pretty light, but I'm getting better at seeing.

Ezra-Dad strides across the cracked-up floor towards a knee-high wall that rings the house. I follow it back and see that the house looks almost exactly the same from the front as it does from the back, apart from having less windows. One of the windows at the top is lying down and the other is tall, making it look like it's winking at me.

I wink back.

Ezra-Dad stops up short, digging his hands in his pocket for something. He bends down and I lift my head up as I slide off his back on to the Outside floor, being careful not to let go of his coat.

I'm standing on the floor – the Outside floor. In my shoes. I can't get more Outside than that.

And then Ezra-Dad moves his arm. And I see what I was afraid of all this time.

We're standing next to a red Dragon.

And I'm brave, just like I knew I would be. I jump, trying to push Ezra-Dad behind me, wielding my empty hands like I'm holding a sword. I ain't strong enough to move Ezra-Dad, but he does show me something shiny in his hand that looks awful like a mini sword, no bigger than a finger.

Well, it ain't what I'd have chosen, but it's better than nothing. I grip hold of his arm and try pushing the sword up to the Dragon, hoping we're finding its heart and piercing it true.

Ezra-Dad shrugs me off, pressing a hidden button on the top of the sword and – *click, click* – the Dragon flashes its fire at the front and the back. Ezra-Dad seems to know what to do, though, as he leans forward, pulls on a scale on the side and opens up a hole right in the beast's belly.

The Dragon stops flashing its fire, just like that.

I'm breathing awful fast, my fists still out and ready to strike.

Ezra-Dad watches me, hands still on the scale he's lifted off the Dragon's side.

I blink the spots from my eyes. 'You OK?' I ask him.

He grunts. 'Will be when ye get in.'

I look at him wide-eyed, and then into the beast's belly again. I take a step back towards the house.

'I ain't getting in no Dragon.'

Ezra-Dad looks at me. He looks at me like I called it by the wrong name. I bite down on my tongue.

'OK,' he says eventually. He jangles his tiny sword again, clicks it at the top, and the Dragon flashes again. 'We'll go somewhere else then. But ye'll have tae walk.'

He starts walking away from me and the Dragon and the house. He has his hands stuffed in his pockets. His shoulders look big, all hunched over like that. He keeps his eyes on the floor like he's afraid it's going to move about.

I dither on the spot, still eyeing up the Dragon. But I don't want to be left alone without Ezra-Dad and his sword, so I take it at a run, catching up to him quick as and clinging to his arm again. He don't stop walking and we go together, out past the wall and into the real-life Outside.

How to be an Outside Person – number four: Go Outside.

FORTY-ONE

I'm walking the whole world. My legs are going forward like they know what to do, but I keep feeling like I need to stop and go back, like any minute now there's going to be a wall in my way.

There ain't, though. There ain't nothing in front of me but grey floor, long and thin like a river, stretching so far that it smudges into the sky. Either side of the river-floor are brown clumps of hair growing up between rocks. I want to go over and touch them, but Ezra-Dad is walking right by them like they ain't nothing important.

There are shapes here and there, too far away for me to see proper, but what look like they might be more houses or sheds. Even more Dragons, all in different colours.

Then I see the mountains.

Mountains are much bigger than I thought. And, when I spin round, I see them all around us, like we're trapped in the bottom of a giant cup. Someone has stirred everything inside so all the grey is mixing in with brown and yellow and – though I can't see much that far – green. Up there, on the mountains.

Green.

I'm breathing awful quick. The cold is making my throat feel scratchy, like there's some invisible hands in this Outside air that want to reach down inside of me and grab at my insides. I try keeping my mouth closed, but the fingers still poke in through my nostrils.

I hold on to Ezra-Dad's arm like it's my sword.

As we walk, one of the bigger shapes up ahead gets clearer. Clear enough to see that it's a house not so different to the one Ezra-Dad and Willow live in. It's got the same windows – one tall and one short – and has a wall going round it, too, though this one looks like it's been eaten in places by big teeth. And it looks sadder, somehow. All dirty and worn. It's dark inside. The windows are covered in dirt and there are more cracks in the floor here than just about anywhere else I've seen.

'What's this place?' I say, my breath panting out of me as I hurry on up next to Ezra-Dad.

'House,' he grunts. 'Empty one. I've been fixing it up for Will.'

We don't stop moving towards it. He leads me past the door that's got red scrawl on it saying *Gaz waz here* and round the side. There's only enough room for one of us at a time down here, so he goes first. I keep a hold of his coat, though. We're squished in between two walls – the house and some other grey one. I keep my eye on the back of his shoes, all blurred as he walks.

How to be an Outside Person – number eighteen: Fix up empty houses.

When we pop out the other end, I have to blink the sun out of my eyes. And, for a moment, I don't even believe that my eyes are open, 'cause right there – right in front of us – is a real-life *tree* growing up out of the grey.

I start breathing hard again. I clutch at Ezra-Dad's shoulder. I push him away. I grab him back.

There's a tree.

'Watch ye –' Ezra-Dad catches me as I throw myself forward so fast I trip. He drags me to my feet. 'Ye kept mentioning trees so ah thought, ye know, seeing that ah just planted it and all . . .'

I shout out all the stuff bubbling up inside of me and I launch myself towards the tree again. It's thin as a twig, a young Maple. I stop just short of it, looking closely at all the scratches round its trunk, all streaked white and brown and green. And I look up and . . . and it's all green. So much green. All fluttering, just like I thought it would. Just like I *knew* it would, and I was right. The trees ain't no story. They ain't dead. They're real. They're real and Ezra-Dad fixed it so it was so.

My chest goes and explodes. I throw my arms round the tree trunk, hugging it close to me and feeling it all scratchy on my face. It smells like . . . like the ground. Like the air. Like the Outside.

'I knew you was real, Maple,' I say, kissing it all over.

The wind blows up my dress and Maple's leaves clatter like hands clapping. She's mine now.

I rub my palms up and down her, feeling at all her dents and scratches and loving each and every one of them.

I look down for her roots, but they're covered over with dirt and trapped in a wall of grey.

I look for Ezra-Dad. He's behind me, looking around with his hands in his pockets.

'You made this?' I gasp at him.

He shakes his head, looking all pink. 'Ah planted it.'

'She's growing? Out of the grey?'

'Well, there's soil under it and I'm gonnae lay a green if ah can lift up the rest of this paving . . . But aye, it's growing.'

I hug her again, hiding my face from Ezra-Dad in case he gets the wrong idea and thinks I'm crying. There are little black dots scurrying all over Maple, all this way and that. They each have little hairs on them and look like ants that begin with A.

'Why'd you say that trees were dead, before?'

I hear him shuffle from foot to foot. 'Well, ah was upset.'

I peek out at him. 'Were you?'

He looks up at the sky. 'Sometimes . . . It's easy tae forget that the whole world didnae die when she did.'

And I know. I thought my whole world died when Zeb did, but I guess it was waiting for me on the other side of those walls after all, just like he always said it was.

I stand for a long time, hugging Maple. Even when I'm feeling itchy from all the black dots. The white light around us starts to turn into grey, and it gets easier to open my eyes and look around. At the big yellow stick that's buried with rocks from the ground. At the round hat next to it. And at the rest of the place, too. The bit of string tied from a pole to the house. More scribbles on the walls that I can't read. Empty cans and packets trodden into the floor.

'Ele? It's raining.'

Raining.

I can feel it dropping on to my hand. On to my face. Dripping into my eye. I look up and watch the drops getting faster and faster, not blue like the rain in the books, but not stinging my eyes neither. I stick out my tongue and taste clouds.

Din I say? Din I say that I was gonna find me some real rain?

'Ele, we should go.'

I sniff. 'Will Maple be OK?'

Ezra-Dad grunts, taking my arm away from her. 'That's how it drinks.'

I knew that.

As he leads me back round the house, I keep looking back at her drinking up all that rain until I can't see no more but grey again.

FORTY-TWO

I've been Outside.

I saw a tree.

I got rain on my face.

I've never felt more like an Outside Person.

When we get home, I need to run upstairs and pee real bad through all my excitement. I listen to the rain on the windows and imagine Maple having the best of times, dancing about. She's standing up through her walls and growing up into the centre of the world.

Anything can grow in walls, if you plant it real careful. Even people can push their roots in and make themselves real. *Maple*. Maple is real.

I am real.

And so are the flowers Willow got me, though their heads have dropped now like they're going for a walk. They look a bit sad, actually, so I go and put them in the toilet so they can have some water, too.

I watch the last bit of *Scrapheap Challenge* with Ezra-Dad, me sitting on the floor where it's most comfortable. It's one we've seen already, so I don't feel bad about speaking through it.

'Today was a mighty fine day.'

He grunts. I try grunting back, as it's a good noise. I can't do it as well as he can, though.

We sit grunting 'til the sky clears of clouds and all the light leaks out of it. We hear Willow come in and run right upstairs without saying no hello.

'He'll come around,' Ezra-Dad says, watching me scowl at the ceiling.

'I got to let him grow,' I whisper back. Just like them plants in the book Ezra-Dad gave me.

At some point, Ezra-Dad goes out and brings me a tea and himself something called a beer, which smells like toes and has more bubbles than a bath. Soon as he starts drinking it, though, he changes. Starts relaxing back. Frowning less. It's like this beer is a magic potion that lets him be less angry for a while. He won't let me have none, though.

'Yer tae young,' he says, like that's that.

I frown at him. I don't know how he knows how old I am when I don't even know.

He's on his usual chair, laid back with his head resting on the top. The material is all worn away there, like some of it has been sticking to the back of his head all this time. When I look, though, I can't see no white chair in his mess of orange curls.

'What was Willow like when he was a little 'un?' I ask. I lie back on the floor, looking up to the room that Willow's in.

'A bairn,' Ezra-Dad grunts, crossing his fingers over his belly and turning the TV off. There ain't no more shows about scrapheaps on now.

'But what was he *like*.'

'Like a bairn.' He chuckles like he ain't supposed to be.

I roll my eyes. 'I ain't knowing what no bairn is like.'

That shuts him up.

I lift my head. It's damn dark out. There's all these little lights on in the sky that I know to be stars, but I can't see none of them properly from here to wish on. The lamp next to Ezra-Dad is on, washing some of the starlight out on the window. The light makes Ezra-Dad's face look like it's torn in half, with only the bit facing the lamp there at all. He talks like he's still got his whole head, though.

'Most bairns are the same. They come out bawling and keep bawling, until they start teething, and then they start bawling and screaming.'

I pull a face. That sounds terrible. 'Why'd you have one then?'

He turns his head so it's all swallowed up by the shadow apart from a bit of beard and ear. 'It's what she wanted.'

I guess that he's talking about Ashley-Mum again, so I don't say nothing for a while. Nor does he. We just sit listening to the house making its clacky creaking.

And then he does something really weird. He starts talking all on his own.

'Ah know ah don't talk about her. It's hard, ye see. But she wanted him – Will. When we met, she said she hated bairns. Didnae want them.' He looks up at the ceiling. 'Then one day she changed her mind for the both of us.'

I tilt my head back further and stare up with him at the patterns swirling up the light like spoons in tea.

'It was different when he came, though. He was the one who changed my mind about kids. There *was* a lot of bawling. And shit, too. Och.'

My laughs sound funny, lying on my back.

'But it didnae matter somehow.'

'Why din he clean up after himself?'

He starts laughing, too, sounding more relaxed than I've ever heard him. 'Yer having me on. If only! Bairns aren't the best at that. They need a lot of looking after.'

I move my head from side to side and watch the patterns swirl.

'Like what kind of looking after?'

'Well, ye know. Everything. Feeding, changing, bathing, burping . . .'

'And what happens? If they don't get looked after right? Do they not turn out all normal?'

I can hear him shrugging – the brush of his shoulders on the back of the chair. 'Cannae tell ye what normal is, tae be honest.'

'It keeps changing,' I whisper, frowning.

Dads are funny, though. In the books, fathers keep you until they run out of food, try their hardest to leave you all alone in the forest, but are mighty sad when they go and succeed. But that ain't what Ezra-Dad is talking about, is it? He's saying that he did all kinds of things for Willow – stuff that's not in any of the stories I read. Nice stuff. Kind stuff.

Maybe that's the difference between being a father and being a dad? The looking after. Even when they're as big of a nuisance as Willow is.

I push myself up on to my elbows and look at Ezra-Dad. He's smiling at something on his finger. There ain't nothing on there that I can see, though.

I take a deep breath and hold it.

'Can you be my dad?' I blurt out all at once.

He stops smiling. He blinks. 'Huh?'

'You don't have to if you don't want to,' I say, quick. 'Ain't nothing big.'

He uncrosses his hands and shifts in his chair, making it squeak.

'Won't yer own dad have something tae say about that?'

My heart jumps. 'I don't have no dad.'

He stops shifting about and looks at me. He's silent for a while, and my ears start thumping.

I shouldn't have said that.

'I've been . . . I've been wanting tae ask,' he says finally, sitting forward, putting his beer down on the table. 'Well, needing tae, ah suppose.'

I scrunch up my eyes, trying to think of another question to ask to distract him. My head's all empty.

'Ele,' he says, 'where is it that yer from?'

'Here,' I say, throwing my eyes to the beer, cussing at it silently in my head. I should've known that no magic potion never did nothing all good. It all seems great at first, relaxing and all, then it turns you into someone who asks questions.

'I'm only asking 'cause –'

'Well don't!' I snap, snatching my body up and my knees forward.

He don't move back. He keeps leaning forward, still as

anything. He scratches his hand through his beard and looks out through the dark window. 'There aren't many folk left in these parts now. Just a few of us, spread out. We keep ourselves tae ourselves mostly.' He takes another sip of beer. 'But ye get tae recognize the ones that are here. The way they act. The way they speak.'

I swallow.

'Yer from the Colt Farm, aren't ye?'

Colt?

'No,' I say, backing off.

He holds up his hands. 'It's OK. Ah know what he's like – a piece of work. I'm nae gonnae tell him that yer here. I've nae told the police about ye yet, have ah? Ye dinnae want to go back there, ah understand that.'

'No!' I say, kicking myself back even further, crouching down.

Colt?

'I didnae know he had a daughter, though,' he says, hand scratching in his stupid orange beard again, all grizzly like a Bear.

Breathe. Breathe. I can't breathe.

'No,' I gasp.

The windows are melting. The Inside is creeping into the Outside like poison.

Ezra-Dad looks at me. He looks in my eyes and he sees. 'Yer the spit of him, come tae think of it.'

I gasp in for air, but my lungs ain't working. They're gripped up by my belly. I bend forward, my forehead colliding with the carpet. Air. No air.

Him.

He is my father. My dad.

No.

'Ele?'

I choke on the air that's tangling up like thin little hairs in my throat. I scratch at the floor, digging up the carpet like it's made out of mud, trying to find . . . trying to . . .

No.

He din look after me. He din take care of me and keep me safe.

His hands on me. His lips. My lips.

Our lips.

They always knew, the Others. They saw me looking like Him and they knew we was the same blood.

I ain't Him, though. I ain't. I ain't. I ain't.

'Ele!'

Hands grab my arms and I throw myself up real fast, some of me wanting to hurt, hurt as bad as it hurts inside me, some of me just wanting to get away.

Crack!

My head rings out as it collides with something hard.

It's Him. He's kicked me in the head again –

No.

I ain't there. I ain't there no more. I escaped. I did, Zeb! I got away from Him, just like you wanted to. You hated Him as much as me. Our dad. *Dad.* We din call him that, though, did we? He weren't no dad to us. Just a Him.

Him.

I'm on a floor. There's carpet, all fuzzy like fur. And there's cussing, deep and low like the walls are coming down. Ezra-Dad.

I moan, grabbing my head, and I force myself to look up. Ezra-Dad is swaying about the room, holding his nose like it might fall off at any moment.

I did that.

How to be an Outside Person – number eight: Don't bite people.

I din bite him, but I hurt him, and I reckon that's the same thing.

He's tilting his head back, trying to blink the pain from his eyes.

My head hurts so bad and my lungs are still squeezing themselves all wrong, all fast, and then –

'What the –'

Willow. At the door. And then there's me, raging like some mad Dragon, seeing red. And Ezra-Dad, hurting.

Look what I've done.

I'm an Other again. I ain't no Outside Person. I certainly ain't Him. I ain't *never* being no spit of Him. I'm them. I'm an Other and I left them.

And I'm so sorry I left them. I'm so *sorry*.

'Ele?' Willow says from behind me.

I'm in a ball. It's dark here. His hands try to prise me out, but I don't come.

'Ele?' he says – someone says.

I'm so sorry.

FORTY-THREE

I'm in a dark place. It smells of me.

I reckon I know where I am, truth be told. I'm right at the entrance to the Outside Inside my Head. Trees are just on the other end of the silence. Jack will be waiting for me on his rock, water running over his toes.

I ain't going through, though. Jack is knocking to me, but I ain't answering. He told me I can't be there no more, and he's right. I left them and I know what that means.

I'm alone.

And there's something else, too. Ezra-Dad and Willow are somewhere behind me, speaking like they're on the other side of a door, all quiet. And I want to listen.

'Dad, would you . . . just let me do this, OK?'

'Ah keep telling ye, I'm *fine*.'

'How'd you get beaten up by a girl, anyway?'

'Ah didnae get beaten up, Will. It was an accident. Her head . . .'

Silence.

'Seriously, though. You OK?'

Sniff. Some kind of moving around. Squeaks on a chair.

'I'm fine. It's her I'm worried about.'

Silence.

'She . . . she's from that Colt Farm. Did ye know?'

'What?' Willow's voice sounds gravelly. 'She told you that?'

'Aye. Well, nae. But her accent . . . I've been thinking it for a while and . . . ah asked.'

Silence.

'She didn't tell me . . .'

Tapping of fingers on the floor, like rain gathering up a storm.

'Dad . . . We've got to help her.'

'Ah know.'

'I know you don't like interfering, but this –'

'Will! Ah know. I'm agreeing with yer. I'm nae always against ye, ye know.'

Silence.

'Oh. I didn't . . .'

Things are so quiet I can hear the house whispering.

'Look. It doesnae matter. What matters is that we give this lassie some help. There are things about her . . .'

'Aye.' Willow's voice, but quiet.

And that's it, ain't it? They know who I am now. I ain't no Outside Person. Even with my hair all gone, all the words I know, and even Maple, they know.

There are things about me that ain't normal.

But here's something they don't know: I've escaped from all that before. And this time the door ain't locked.

FORTY-FOUR

I'm running real fast on a black sea.

The air is blowing my dress flat against me and whistling in my ears.

I got my books with me – all three – to my chest like they belong in there, next to my heart.

I ain't gonna make the mistake of forgetting the important stuff. Not again.

I'm sorry.

The moon is a white hole exploded in the sky, showing me the way to escape. I'm wishing on every star I see, even the tiny ones that just look like wall dust.

Make me real. Make me an Outside Person.

I can't see my feet. I might as well be swimming in a big pit of black nothing, for all I feel of myself. I got my shoes on, so I don't feel nothing but the cold numbing up my bones and puddles splashing old rain at my legs. The only pain I got is the one in my chest, and I don't know if that's my heart ripping itself open or my lungs biting its breaths.

I don't stop, though. I can't.

As soon as I heard Willow and Ezra-Dad leave the room, I picked up my books and I left, through the front door, like it weren't nothing.

How to be an Outside Person – number five: Don't think about the Inside.

They know. I broke my rule.

But I'm still gonna be an Outside Person. I ain't going back Inside. I ain't. I was stupid thinking that I could just stay with Willow and Ezra-Dad in their house, living happily ever after. But it's OK. This is my story and I can keep turning over the pages and start again from blank.

I can still run.

My breaths start ripping in and out of me, taking bits of my insides with them. I can feel myself getting smaller and smaller, but it ain't far now. It ain't far.

I'm nearly there. I just got to keep going.

I just got to think on something real.

That's what you do when everything seems as bad as a house made of straw. You gotta make a plan. Think about those truths.

How to be an Outside Person – number one: Don't look at no sun.
How to be an Outside Person – number two: Wear extra-skins clothes.
How to be an Outside Person – number three: Look like them.

How to be an Outside Person – number four: Go Outside.

How to be an Outside Person – number five: Don't think about the Inside.

How to be an Outside Person – number six: Talk to them.

How to be an Outside Person – number seven: Know all the Outside words.

How to be an Outside Person – number eight: Don't bite people.

How to be an Outside Person – number nine: Know someone who's died.

How to be an Outside Person – number ten: Be nice to Giants.

How to be an Outside Person – number eleven: Make music.

How to be an Outside Person – number twelve: Read all the books.

How to be an Outside Person – number thirteen: Go downstairs.

How to be an Outside Person – number fourteen: Make tea.

How to be an Outside Person – number fifteen: Don't spit no food out.

How to be an Outside Person – number sixteen: Eat at the table.

How to be an Outside Person – number seventeen: Have things that are only yours.

How to be an Outside Person – number eighteen: Fix up empty houses.

And, just when my body is thinking of throwing me away, I see it. The house.

I run round the side, where Ezra-Dad took me, until I see her. She's still standing, waiting for me. Like I knew she would.

'Maple!' I gasp, dropping to my knees to hug her base and throwing my ribs out wide to catch all the air on the floor. Her bark feels like my knuckles, all worn from years of knocking on walls.

'We're free now,' I say to her between breaths. 'We're Outside.'

And I feel it. For the first time since I ran out of that Tower, I feel Outside. In my lungs, in my blood and even in my head.

I'm Outside. And I'm alone.

FORTY-FIVE

Footsteps.

I remember when footsteps used to make me feel like I din have no insides. Now they just make me feel lonely. They ain't coming for me.

I'm lying at the bottom of Maple. I was mighty hot when I got here, but it's cold now. I got my coat on, but the wet on the floor has seeped through to my skin.

I got all the wishes I need to keep me alive, though. A whole sky of them. There are more stars than I ever did see in any book, spread as far as I can see all around me. There are moving stars, too, with red lights that flash. I reckon that's a wish on its way to being granted.

I frown. Those footsteps are getting louder. I can feel them in the ground now, rumbling up my bones.

Is it an Ogre?

I jump to my feet and stand in front of Maple. I ain't got no sword, but I got my teeth. I got my nails and my fists.

All I need is me to take down anything.

A big ol' shadow creeps up along the side of the house. It's wheezing and panting so loud that it sounds like it's the size of the house.

I don't stop to think. I pick up a stone from the floor and I throw it as hard and as far as I can towards it.

And *crack!*

It hits the wall of the house, bouncing right in the path of the beast, who screams out loud and says, 'Ele! What the hell?'

Willow.

I back up against Maple and pick up another rock. 'Stay away!'

Willow puts out his hand. The whites of his eyes shine like moons. He backs up.

'You're really fast,' he says, still panting. His hands are on his knees now, but he's still looking at me.

'I ain't going back!' My stupid voice is all crackly.

He shakes his head. 'Put the rock down so we can talk properly.'

I look at the rock. 'I can fight you, you know.'

Willow lets his head drop, so he's almost squatting on the floor. 'Aye. I believe that.'

I frown, but I drop the rock.

He stumbles towards me like his legs ain't his, still coughing and wheezing. He sits down near to me and fumbles in his pocket for a blue stick, which he sticks in his mouth, clicks and then breathes from.

I watch him as he holds his breath. His eyes are closed. Then he lets the breath out, before falling on to his back. He sees me looking at the blue stick in his hand.

'What?' he says. 'I have asthma, OK? It's an inhaler.'

I watch him, not sure whether to run away again or not.

He flails an arm to his right. 'Sit. The ground's not that wet.'

I do sit, slowly, being careful to squat so I can get up again and start running if I need to.

'Why'd you follow me?' I ask.

'What, you think I was just going to let you take off into the night alone?' He shakes his head. 'Where are we, anyway? Whose house is this?'

We look together at the broken-up house, all its windows dark and covered with writing that don't make no sense.

'It's Ezra-Dad's.'

'Huh?' Willow says, sitting up, his frown back. 'Dad already has a house.'

I shrug. 'He said it was his. He's "fixing it up" for you, or something.'

Willow shakes his head. 'He wouldn't do that for me . . .' He swallows. 'Look, I'm sorry for getting angry. Before, I mean.' He shoots me a look out of the corner of his eye. 'I just . . . I mean, you see him as this . . . this amazing guy, and he's not. I just thought you'd get that.'

I sigh.

Willow starts tapping again. Real fast on his knees. And, when he speaks, it all comes out of his mouth at once. 'You see him as this great dad. And he is to *you*, but he should be to *me*.'

Even in the dark, I can see his face is red.

'He's your dad, Willow. Yours. You don't even know how lucky you are, do you? I'd give all my toes to have a dad like yours. You got two castles and a whole Kingdom.'

Willow is looking at me weirdly.

'You have all of this and you don't even know it's the best thing ever.'

He opens his mouth to say something, but nothing comes out.

I close my eyes and face the sky. The leaves of Maple are making shadows like fingers on my eyes.

'I'm sorry,' he says eventually. 'For storming out that time. And then ignoring you. I'm a jerk.'

I nod and he sighs.

'Look, I'm trying to help you. Can you at least tell me what's wrong? Why'd you run away?'

''Cause you hate me,' I whisper. ''Cause I ain't from here and I don't know everything, and you know now and –'

'Ele,' Willow says, but I don't look at him. He pulls my chin over to him, but I keep my eyes screwed up closed so I can't see all the hate in his eyes.

'It's fine. I don't know anything, either. We just . . . we figure it out together as we go along.'

I peek at him. He's looking at me with eyes like the night sky.

We don't say nothing for a good long time. The night is still, like someone has stopped time. We lie down together, though, and it's warm next to him.

'Do you know why I stopped playing the Angus game?' Willow says after a while.

I don't say nothing back, just keep on staring into the stars.

'It's 'cause Dad tried to play it with me. Stupid, huh? I was out in the garden most days after Mum died, making myself believe I was fighting pirates rather than dealing with all the crap that goes with suddenly having a dead mum.'

I hear the scrape of his head on the ground as he shakes it.

'Dad would watch me from the kitchen window. And then, one day, he came outside. He put his hand on my head and he said, in that awkward way of his, "Um, it's nice tae meet ye, Angus." And he put out his other hand like he was shaking hands with him, and Angus was up a tree or something at the time and . . . I don't know. I just got angry.'

He swallows and I take his hand. It's cold, but he squeezes mine back.

'I just started screaming at Dad. I don't remember what I said, but it was really, really bad stuff. Angus was mine. Mine, away from him and all the crap that was going on. And he came in and ruined it.

'I didn't play with Angus after that. Not ever. And Dad and I didn't talk about it, either. We didn't talk at all, really. And, I don't know . . . Maybe I was angry at him for not trying. And then angry at you for not being all mine, too.' He sighs.

I shift about. 'I'm not Angus.'

Willow nods. 'Aye, I know.'

I tilt my head 'til it rests against his shoulder.

'I wish I was,' I whisper.

But Willow shakes his head again. 'You're Ele. And that's the best person to be.'

We're still for a while. All the thoughts about what makes me who I am are whirling around inside of me, waiting to come out.

The Inside.

The Outside.

Zeb.

The Others.

Jack.

Him. My dad.

My mouth is clamped shut, but my chest is awful sick of churning it all around in the dark.

How to be an Outside Person – number five: Don't think about the Inside.

But maybe I want to think about them. And maybe I want to tell Willow. Maybe I want him to see me for who I am, after all. Who I *really* am. Not as just some name that don't mean nothing. Not as Ele from that Colt Farm.

'Let me tell you a story,' I say, all quiet. 'About before I met you. About . . . about where I was. Who I was with.'

'Uh-huh?' he says.

I lick my lips. 'Once upon a time, there was a girl who lived in a Tower.'

And I tell him. About the Others. I tell him about each one of them, about how they liked me and how they din. I tell him about how Queenie was, and about how sweet Bee could be. I tell him about Cow being greedy, about Jack, my friend, knocking on the walls, and how it felt like everything died when Zeb did.

I tell him and he holds my hand.

I try saying about Him – about the bad bits – but my voice goes and runs out then.

When I break off, Willow don't say nothing for a while. It takes me a few minutes to realize that he's asleep.

It don't matter none, though. I said it all. And saying it out loud felt even better than hiding away from it. 'Cause it always finds you, don't it?

How to be an Outside Person – number five: Don't think about the Inside.
How to be an Outside Person – number five: Tell the truth.

FORTY-SIX

I slept Outside last night. The whole night, curled up round Maple and Willow – my very own two trees. And I dreamt about *her* like she was with us, too.

She was reading to us. A story. Her voice was soft, like a whisper. Those red lips were smiling as she was speaking the words.

'Hansel pushed the old Witch into the oven and slammed the door closed. The Witch screamed and disappeared into the fire, never to be seen again. Hansel released his sister, and together they found their father, who was wandering in the woods looking for them, having left his evil wife. They all moved into the gingerbread house, never to go hungry again.'

And my hands were clapping and I was calling for her to read the bit about the sugar windows again, my feet kicking Zeb's, who was sitting on her other leg. But he was frowning.

She stroked her hand across his forehead. His hair was so short that it stroked her fingers back.

'Was that a bit too scary?' she asked him.

But Zeb just looked at the door. A white door. Closed.

'We could push Him in the oven,' he said.

And her fingers stopped playing with his hair. She froze up like wall.

She had blue eyes. Yellow hair. Just like ours.

Her voice lost the whisper. Now it was a hiss. 'Never, ever say that again. Do you hear me?'

And those blue eyes were full of fear.

I stopped clapping. She looked from Zeb to the door, her red lips trembling. Then she caught my wide eyes.

She pulled us both close, that red smile back like it never went away. 'Now. How about another story?'

And she opened the book again and started reading. But all the time Zeb was looking at me. Looking like he knew something I din.

I reckon I know now, though.

That lady with the red lips, she was our mother. And she was so scared that she was frozen to the spot when she should have been running. With us. Far away from Him.

'Cause it was Him she was afraid of, weren't it? And I know. I know that.

But I ain't gonna let no fear stop me running. Never again.

I'm an Outside Person now. I can feel that as truth, burning bright inside me. But I got to set some things right if I'm gonna really do this.

I'm gonna have to be as brave as I ever was to do it.

Seems to me that I need myself a new set of rules.

How to set things right – number one: Say sorry.

First thing I got to do is quit being so stupid and pushing people away. I got to cling on to all the best things and keep them safe on a shelf, like my books.

I'm up before even the sun's up properly. It's just stretching its fingers over the horizon, so everything looks kind of dim. I untangle myself from Willow's hand and leave him sleeping next to Maple. He looks younger somehow, without the frowning or the smiling.

I walk back to Willow's house with my books in my hands. The air feels wet and my dress is as cold as walls. I soon warm up, though, and I make it back without needing to stop once, even though my legs are calling out for a rest by the time I let myself in the front door.

It's still dark inside. I don't want to turn on the lights yet, so I keep the shadows on.

Making porridge in the almost-dark when you ain't made it on your own before is hard going. I manage to get it in the bowl all right, but I go and forget the milk that'll make it up, so it burns down black in the microwave.

We ain't got no more porridge, and the kitchen's looking even more dim on account of all the smoke in it, but I ain't letting that stop me. I got some making-up to do, and breakfast seems as good a way of doing it as any. I keep thinking of Ezra-Dad's face last night, all covered in hurt.

They need to know I'm better than all of that.

I open up the can cupboard and look for stuff that sounds like it might be for breakfast. None of it says it on the cans. It's all stuff I'm damn sure we've had for dinner before. I find three cans at the back, though, all dusty. On the front is a picture of a circle with an egg on top, and once Ezra-Dad gave me an egg for breakfast. When I open the can, it don't look like the eggs he made, though. The can says 'SPAM' on it, and the pink stuff inside is round and flat, nothing like an egg at all.

I hold the can upside down and it makes a squelch as it plops out. I put the plates on the table and go upstairs – all on my own – and fetch the flowers from out of the toilet. I put them in a jug I find under the kitchen sink, and place it in the middle of the table, just like the flowers in 'Goldilocks and the Three Bears'.

My stomach is rumbling up a storm now, so I make plenty of noise getting together the tea. Pretty soon I hear the pipes washing down from upstairs. Ezra-Dad.

I guess you could say I'm excited. I spill hot water over the worktop and burn my fingers red. But it looks nice – food on the table with the flowers, tea all there in the middle in its own little pot for everyone to just help themselves to. I put the knives and forks down by the plates like Willow showed me. I hear Ezra-Dad plodding down the stairs, so I quickly yank out my chair and sit down at the table.

I put my hands on my plate. I sit back and put them on my lap. I sit forward and grip the table.

The front door bangs shut and Willow stumbles in at the same moment as Ezra-Dad. Willow's clothes are all crumpled and his eyes are squinting out. He swears under his breath when he sees me, then plonks himself down in a chair, breathing from his inhaler again. He looks mighty pleased to see me.

Ezra-Dad is beaming.

'What's all this?' he shouts, and he ain't saying it to the smoke in the air, or the porridge on the floor, or the water dripping down from the worktop. He's saying it to me and the stuff I gone and put out for them.

I feel myself blushing up all hot. 'I wanted to say sorry. For hurting you and all.'

Ezra-Dad smiles so wide his beard touches his hair. He sits himself down, too. 'Well, that's magic. Will?'

Willow ain't listening. He points at his plate, still huffing and puffing. 'What's this?'

I bite my lip. 'Spam-eggs. Is it not right?'

He breaks into a big smile, too, putting his inhaler back in his pocket and taking his coat off.

'No, it's great! I love spam. I didn't even know we had any.'

I beam at him, watching him tuck in. Ezra-Dad is raising his eyebrows at the numbers on the top of the can that say *31–10–2016*, but when he sees me looking all concerned he picks up his fork and tucks in, too.

Ezra-Dad and Willow are my favourite Outside People in the world.

I stab my spam-egg right in the belly with my fork and bite on it whole. It's kind of like feed, if feed was made into hunks from cans. I spit it out. 'This is horrible.'

Willow and Ezra-Dad exchange glances, laughing, but they keep on eating. I raise an eyebrow at both of them and drink my tea to take away the taste.

They're my favourite Outside People, but they're weird.

FORTY-SEVEN

I find Willow staring out of the window upstairs when I knock on the door.

'Oh.' He spins round. 'Sorry. I'm in your room.'

I shrug, sitting down on the bed. 'It's your room, really.'

'It's OK. I kind of like the one next door.' He stretches his back, grimacing. 'Much better than sleeping on the bloody pavement, anyway.'

I smile. 'Thanks for coming to find me.'

He sidles up beside me on the bed, with one foot tucked under him so he's facing me. 'I've been trying to remember what you said last night . . .'

My heart kicks. So he was awake, then. I look away from him, trying to hide my face from him with my own shoulder.

'I'm pleased. That you told me, I mean.' I feel his hand on mine, lightly touching, not quite holding. 'I was kind of asleep and don't remember all of it, but, like, it's nice to know that you have a family, you know?'

I let my shoulders down. 'Family?'

'You know, the, er . . . Others? Bee, Queenie. Cowell, was it? Anyway, they sound nice.'

'Cow,' I say, turning to face him fully now. Just him saying their names, saying them out loud in the light, is making my belly twang with something that I don't know if it is missing or guilt, or both of them all mixed up.

'Cow. Right,' he says, nodding. Then he frowns. 'What is that, like a nickname or something?'

I shrug.

'Aye, well. I'd like to meet them someday.'

I take a deep breath in. 'That's actually why I came in.' My voice sounds all scratched up, but I ain't scared. I ain't.

How to set things right – number two: Be brave.

Willow frowns slightly. 'Aye?'

'Aye,' I say. 'I mean, yeah.'

OakWillowBirchSycamore.

'Willow,' I say. 'I got to go back.'

My heart is beating up inside of me like it's desperate to get out. But I ain't closing my ears to it no more. I hear those knocks.

'Right,' Willow says, looking to the door. 'But Dad said that you lived at the Colt place.'

Colt. I grip the blanket tighter.

Willow waits for me to give him some kind of sign that he's right, but I can't do that.

'Right . . . Well, I'm guessing there's a reason you ran away. And, to be honest, I've seen him around and – no offence – but he's really weird. Like, *really.*' He rubs his hand over his chin, like Ezra-Dad does, but he ain't got no beard to tangle his fingers in. 'Like, this one time, I took my bike up there to the farm and, you know, started just looking around, whatever. Anyway, he caught me trying to break into a stone barn, and he chased me out of there with a gun.' His eyes go wide. 'No joke.'

My heart is beating so fast now that I can't even feel it. I'm floating up somewhere on the ceiling, looking down at Willow telling these tales. Not thinking. Not thinking about how he would've been on just the other side of my wall. My Prince. No – not thinking about that.

ChestnutAshPine.

'I got . . . I got to show you.' I open my mouth to say more, but I ain't got nothing.

Willow licks his lips. 'Your family, they're still there, aren't they? With him?'

Still I don't say nothing. I can't. I ain't got no words.

He stares at me. 'You want to go rescue them?'

And suddenly his eyes are all fire.

'I can help you! I can go in. You can just, you know, show me where they are. And maybe keep a lookout?' He stands up and marches to the window. 'I can rescue them.'

I'm somewhere up on that ceiling still, floating.

He turns round and looks at me with those dark eyes of his. Seeing me and not seeing me at all.

Not yet, anyway.

I watch myself nod in his eyes. They spark. He starts pacing around.

'We'll take the car. The farm's only across the way, but it'll give us a quicker getaway if he sees us.'

He won't see us.

'I'll get Dad's crowbar from the shed, and maybe a knife or something. Or do you think that's too much?'

I stare at him.

'Aye, too much. We'll wear black, though, and go later, when it gets dark. Harder to spot us that way, right? Oh, and –' he squats down in front of me – 'probably best not to tell Dad, OK? He'll just . . . complicate things.'

'Lie?' I croak.

He sighs. 'No, not *lie*. Just . . . don't tell him the truth. Different things.'

'Different things,' I whisper. 'Right.'

There are so many rules to this Outside that sometimes I can't keep up.

He smiles, holding me in his eyes.

'This is going to be good. Really good.'

FORTY-EIGHT

Ain't no use being scared of time. It comes on forward in any case, whether you're afraid of it or not.

We got the whole day at the beginning. The sun is shining and it seems like it ain't never getting dark. But then, soon enough, we're having our lunch and I'm staring at my food while Willow chats to Ezra-Dad like he's his bestest friend, and I'm too mixed up to enjoy the look of happy surprise on Ezra-Dad's face.

I'm trying to keep everything balled up in my hands, as perfect as it is. The eyes that Willow looks at me with when we're elbow-deep in washing-up bubbles. The happy humming coming from the living room when Ezra-Dad empties the bins. The feeling of being warm and on soft things and having a full belly. But it's all trickling on through my fingers.

It's time, though. It's the right thing to do.

'Mind if I go practise?' Willow says from behind me, drying his hands on the cloth I know to be a tea towel.

I shake my head. 'Can I listen in?'

He smiles. 'Sure.'

We go into his old room, my new one. I sit on the bed as he wakes up his music stand and rests a book on top called *Violin Exam Pieces: Grade 7.*

'What do those letters mean?' I ask, peering over at the little black blobs all caught up in lines of spiderwebs.

'They're notes,' he says, twiddling on the keys sticking out of the violin's nose. 'Each one means a different kind of sound.'

I frown. 'Ain't like no notes I ever did see.'

Willow shrugs. 'Aye, not everyone uses them. I have to for my exam, but it's better to learn it by heart anyway.'

He strokes his bow over the strings on the violin and it starts singing. I lie back, closing my eyes. For a while, he just goes up and down with his sounds, like we're climbing trees made out of music notes. They go up, higher and higher, before coming back down again, one branch at a time. I can almost see that note writing in the sounds he makes, using the lines of the spiderweb to climb from the bottom to the top.

Then he starts playing proper. Something slow at first. He keeps stopping and muttering to himself, then going back and making the same sounds again. I like to watch him play. When he feels me watching him, he's all smiley and jokey, but when he forgets I'm there he frowns. Closes his eyes. Sways. It's like seeing him with my eyes closed.

I start recognizing the tune a bit, and hum it out as he plays.

He stops, smiling again – as much as he can, with his chin all smushed into the violin, anyway.

'You're singing the cello part, did you know?'

Now, I din know that. But I like the idea of having music inside of me that I din even know I had.

When he's done with the slow song, he starts playing something else. Something fast. Something that has him dancing from left to right as his arm swoops from side to side and up and down. The music bounces off the walls and has me sitting up, smiling, my feet bouncing along like they're running on music.

'Come on!' Willow shouts, spinning round in a circle and bouncing from foot to foot. I get up and copy him, though it's difficult without a violin to play myself. I hop from one foot to the other. Spin round. I start slow, but I get caught up in all the music and my feet start working on their own. They tap out from side to side. My arms swing about. I jump up high. Go down low. And spinspinspin.

It's like running with Zeb again. I can almost feel him dancing next to me and I reckon it's the first time I felt him since I left his stain on the floor of the Inside. I close my eyes and I breathe him in.

Willow dances around me, ducking and weaving. Now and again we catch each other's eye all in a blur and we smile with our teeth.

The song ends on a big, long note and I fall down. My face pushes into the bed and catches all my breaths. I feel Willow flop down next to me.

'Phew! Ah, that's a fun one.'

I pull my head to the side so I can see him. He's smiling wide at the ceiling, pulling in breaths from his inhaler.

'Irish,' he says, catching my eye. 'They know how to dance.'

How to be an Outside Person – *number nineteen: Dance like the Irish.*

We lie together, eating up the air until it's time for him to practise some more slow songs again. I stay lying down, though, watching him.

When Willow leaves, I get myself up and sit by the window, looking out at the night closing in from above, like I'm one of the clouds. The shed is looking mighty small now, like a dent in the floor of the world. And I remember the time when that was the biggest thing I ever did see, so it gets me wondering just how small that Tower really is.

Ain't nowhere to hide in a small place.

And that's OK. I'm done with hiding from Willow, anyway. He says he wants to know all this stuff about who I am, like he wants to see me with his eyes closed, too. I don't reckon it'll be as beautiful as him playing on that violin, but it'll be the truth. That's probably the best thing I got to give him.

And, anyway, I got to do this. I can't live the truth when I'm still carrying lies. I know that now.

'I ain't scared. I ain't scared. I ain't.' I say it into the window until all my breath disappears the view Outside.

'Ready?' Willow says from behind me, dressed in black like a shadow.

I wipe the window clear and stand up.

'Ready.'

PART THREE

INSIDE

FORTY-NINE

It seems that stealing a car is the most exciting thing anyone could ever do, by the way Willow is acting.

That's what they call Dragons: cars.

We're squatting near the red one outside the house. Willow looks more alive than I ever did see him, bending low and looking over to the front window of the house, which I guess Ezra-Dad is sitting behind. We can't see in, though – the curtains are closed. The light coming through them makes Willow's eyes seem like they're lighting up from the inside.

It's awful dark out here. The air is as cold as I ever felt, and I have to wrap my arms round myself to stop shaking. I can hear things, too. A distant roar, like when you cup your hands over your ears. And I can see lights up on the mountains far away, all blurred together like lines of fire.

OakWillowBirchSycamore.

Willow turns to smile at me. 'Let's go.'

He runs silently round the Dragon-car. I hear a small tap and it flashes its fire again – *click, click* – all yellow.

***How to be an Outside Person – number twenty: Don't be
afraid of Dragon-cars.***

I duck down when Willow does, waiting for Ezra-Dad to
look out of that window and ask what we're up to. He don't.

The floor feels as cold as a fridge under my hands.

There's another light as Willow opens the scale on the side
of the Dragon-car. I can still see him through its big glassy
eye as he slides in and moves something. The Dragon-car
starts to roll silently. My eyes are wide. They watch Willow
walk the Dragon-car like a horse down the hill from the
house.

He looks at me, tilting his head to tell me to come over.
Some of me wants to stay here in the shadow of the house,
where things ain't so bad. Where I can cook breakfast, and
people will eat it who look at me like I belong here. Like I'm
a normal Outside Person.

But I go with him.

The Dragon-car looks different all up close. Inside, I can
see seats and buttons, and it has windows and doors, too, like
the Dragon-car ain't nothing more than another type of
house on wheels.

'What is this?' I whisper.

'A hunk of junk is what it is,' Willow hisses. 'Get in.'

Not a Dragon-car at all, then.

There's a black thing on it that looks kind of like a door
handle. I touch it, half-expecting it to be all hot from Dragon
fire, but it's as cold as taps. I pull it up and the door opens.

'Get in!' Willow says again.

The hunk of junk is still moving, but I manage to climb in on my knees, kneeling up on the seat. It smells of carpet inside.

The hunk of junk stops rolling and Willow slides in, too, on the other side. His door closes.

'Close your door,' he says.

I look at the Outside through the crack in the door. I shake my head.

Willow sighs, leans over me and spins another handle round. The window opens into a hole big enough for a girl to slide on out of if she needed to.

I close the door. The light inside goes off.

He lets out all his breath at once. It clouds inside the hunk of junk like tea steam.

'Nice,' he whispers. 'I don't think he saw.'

He looks at me, his wide grin showing all his teeth. I hear him fumble around under the wheel, his eyes unfocused. Then the hunk of junk comes to life all at once. The lights inside come flashing on, the insides start shaking and the noise rumbles right through that silence.

I grip the side of the door, throwing a look back to the living-room window, where the curtains are twitching.

'He's there!' I shout, my heart up in my throat.

Willow is all arms. He moves the stick in the middle forward and we're thrown forward, too – once, twice – hopping like we're running downstairs.

'Shit,' Willow says, but he's still smiling.

The hunk of junk gets louder and louder, and Willow whoops over its roars. We're going so fast that I can't move myself out of the chair. I clutch at the door. Willow laughs, hitting the wheel and rocking backwards and forwards in his seat.

'Stop!' I say, looking down at my white fingers.

'Huh?'

'STOP!' I shout louder.

'Yeah, sure. I guess it makes sense to walk up, anyway. You're right.'

He lets the hunk of junk roll to the side. We hit a bump and my head slams into the back of the chair. Then we stop.

'OK?' Willow says, putting his hand on my shoulder.

I nod, not really seeing him. I'm too busy looking at the black squares up on the hill in front of us.

'You want to stay here?' he asks.

I lick my lips. I do. I really do.

'I ain't scared,' I whisper. I open the door, stepping back out into the cold and dark like it ain't nothing.

Willow gets out and leans over the top of the hunk of junk, still smiling at me. His eyes are all black.

'We'll go up slowly, OK? Keep out of sight. You just need to show me where they are, that's all.'

I nod and clench my fists, all buried up in my sleeves.

That's all.

FIFTY

I already know we're in the right place before I see the rusted-up sign saying *Colt Farm*. It's nailed to a post tangled up with spiky wire and leaning like it's been kicked in the belly.

Willow flicks it as we walk by, making a short hollow noise. A noise that reminds me of feed hitting the feed bowl.

My legs feel empty, but they're walking. We follow a grey path, the wire all trodden into the ground and tangled up round other posts like fingers caught in hair. The floor is the same grey as we've got at our house – *our* house – but cracked up, like Giants have been jumping on it. In between the cracks is something softer, drier. Like dirt.

I'm looking for something familiar, but I don't remember it at all from when I ran away all them days ago. All I got is the feeling of bad weighing in my belly, like I'm carrying a hunk of metal right inside my guts.

As we move, Willow walks closer to me, putting his hand behind my back. I'm wondering if he can feel it, too.

Bad things happen here. It's in the air, buzzing.

One of the shapes is a hunk of junk. It's bigger than Ezra-Dad's one, wheels the size of tables, and it's got seats upstairs. It has a room in the back with a roof of black.

I know that hunk of junk, but I don't know how I do. I can feel it moving, though, in the palms of my hands and my knees. I can see yellow light flashing in from the sides. I can hear small whimpers from behind me.

And red lips, too. Red lips not smiling.

I walk as far away from it as I can.

There are things all around. Lots of things, all metal. They're planted like flowers, sticking up as sharp as knives. Some of them have writing on them, like the numbers stuck on the front of the hunk of junk. And there's big things, too. Big round discs with spikes on them. A cupboard with hundreds of boxes in it. Long, crooked bars.

'OK?' Willow asks as we walk past a load of hooks hanging from a metal roof, swaying like someone is pushing them towards us.

I manage to nod.

'Some farm, eh?' Willow laughs, but he ain't really smiling.

I don't answer. I just walk us up the hill, my legs cussing. Buildings loom into view, one looking like Willow's house but smaller and darker, windows grubby and locked up. He pulls me away, towards other buildings further on, but I keep looking back. I can't help it.

There's a house here. A real house, with windows and doors and a roof. It has windows. Painted-up doors that look like they'd open with a kick. I can see shapes behind the windows. A kettle. Washing-up liquid. Curtains.

I stop. Turn round. And I walk back to that house.

'Ele? Ele, come on. We can't stay here. He might see.'

The windows are all dark and dirty – not as bad as the ones on the house Ezra-Dad took me to see, but bad enough to make it difficult to see through. I climb the step under the door on the side of the house, a door that kind of looks like Willow's back door, but without the wood bit across the middle. This one is full of glass, all swirled up so you can't see in.

The handle is cold. It squawks when I push it down.

'Ele! What the hell are you doing?' Willow calls in a whisper. He ain't moved to the house with me.

My heart is all up in my throat. I swallow it down when I push the door open and step inside.

'Holy shit. It's unlocked,' Willow says, his footsteps behind me now.

It's dark inside, only bits of moon lighting up what looks like a kitchen. It ain't as nice as Willow's, though. The floor is covered with bits that snap as I tread on them – bits of food or glass or something. It don't smell like Him, but it don't smell nice, neither. It smells old. Left. Like bins and old coats.

But there are cupboards. There's a table with a bottle on it. There's a load of cups and plates in the sink, all with bits of dinner on them.

His dinners. His.

'Was this your house?' Willow says, still behind me.

I shake my head. If I thought really hard, I could imagine it being mine. My table, where I'd eat my porridge. My kettle, where I'd make myself tea. My floor, covered in leaves from the forest. They're the things crunching up as I walk.

'We should go,' Willow says.

I walk through the door to a room with stairs leading upward. I can see another door up ahead – a beat-up wooden one that's breathing out the cold of the Outside. I walk towards it and catch myself in a mirror hanging on the wall. It's square and peeling up at one corner. My face and eyes look so white they're shining.

'Ele?' Willow says.

I turn away from the girl in the mirror and start walking upstairs.

'Ele!' Willow hisses, and I can hear the panic in his voice now. Hear it shaking, like my insides are starting to do. But not yet. Not yet.

I walk up. The banister ain't painted white like Willow's. There ain't no carpet on the stairs, neither. It's all wood, and my shoes make hollow noises as they climb.

When I get to the top, I find what I'm looking for.

I grip the banister so tight that the bones in my hand start cussing. But there, ahead of me, are three rooms. I can see a bed poking from behind the door in the room dead ahead. There are clothes all around, and bottles, too. I recognize a lamp. A phone. Trousers on the floor.

I stop looking in that room. One of the other rooms has the door closed. It's an ugly brown door, with a metal handle like the cold one Outside. The other room has its door swung wide, but I can't see no bed in it. Just a white cage with a stuffed-up and dead Bear trapped inside it.

'Is this where they are?' Willow whispers. 'The Others?'

I shake my head and, as I do, all the feeling that I been keeping out of me comes rushing in like water from a tap. I squeeze my fists, turn right round, and run down the stairs as fast as my stupid legs will let me, which ain't fast enough. The wood from the banister bites at the scabs on my hands as I slide them down. I stumble and crash into the wall at the bottom.

The girl in the mirror is screaming out her silence.

Willow runs behind me, out of the kitchen, out of the side door and back out into the night. Out and out and out, until my legs are shaking so much that they ain't moving forward no more.

Willow pushes me lightly on the back, urging me on. I stumble up, keeping my head down and scrunching my face up.

Goddamn. Goddamn.

My fingernails dig into my palms.

Willow drags me round a small building made of wood, and sits me on an upturned bucket so I'm hidden from the house. I stick my head in between my hands, squeezing my skull between my fists, panting.

And then I scream. Scream and howl and empty all the everything inside of me.

That goddamn man. Fuck Him. *Fuck Him.*

'Ele! Are you OK? Ele, speak to me.'

I shake my head. I ain't got no words. No words.

Three rooms. *Three.*

I'd thought maybe – *maybe* – He din have no room for us. Maybe that was why He did it. 'Cause He din have no choice.

'He had a choice!' I yell into the night.

I bend over, breathing like there ain't no air.

'Had what choice?' Willow's hands are on my shoulders. He's looking around for eyes in the dark. 'Maybe this was a bad idea . . .'

I shake my head. Shake it too long, so I know I'm being mighty weird, but it's the only thing stopping me going back up to that house and smashing every single one of those windows with my own fists.

'No,' I gasp out, and I stand shakily. I can't look him in the eye, but I know how he's looking at me. Scared. Scared of me.

But he needs to see. Now more than ever. We both do.

I push him ahead of me.

'You sure?'

Goddamn him for trying to look at my face. I push him forward, away from me, nodding as best I can.

We walk until the ground levels out. The clouds move in the sky and the moon makes everything glow blue.

It sees me, the moon. It sees me for what I am and it don't blink.

So I look out, too. I look past Willow's shoulder, past all the broken-down buildings with no walls that hold heaps of more metal junk. Past the wooden sheds, the spiky wire, the cracked-up floor. And I see it: the Tower. My house. And I don't blink.

FIFTY-ONE

'We don't have to do this if you don't want to.'

I don't want to. But we do.

My breathing has gone mighty strange. It's all whine, like something is dying right inside me. I want to stop making the noise. I want to, but I can't.

It's all I have to keep me moving forward.

Willow walks in front of me, forced on by my own hands. It's good to have something to hold on to. Something real.

The Tower don't look like any of the other buildings. It ain't made of metal, for one. It's made of wall, just like I remember. And it has doors, made to keep people out as well as in. It's bigger than the house, but made long and thin, like a hallway.

'It looks like a stable or something. You sure this is right?'

It's right.

We keep walking.

There's two doors – one at each end. I ain't sure which one I came out of, but I march up to the closest one.

If I don't think about it, I could be dreaming. The moon is making everything unreal, anyway. Shadows poke into the nooks and crannies of the walls, and up on the triangle roof. There's a round box on the side that looks like a massive pill, pipes going off into the walls and disappearing.

Everything is so quiet.

We stop outside the door and I'm suddenly thankful for Willow's dithering. He turns to me, wrapping an arm over my shoulders and looking at me all concerned. It ain't how it's supposed to be. I'm the brave one here. I am.

'You don't have to go in, you know.'

I do. I know I do.

How to set things right – number two: Be brave.

I nod. And I guess that's all the brave I have.

He grabs the handle and opens the door easily, revealing a long room and an almighty bad smell.

'Och.' Willow coughs. 'What is that?'

I push him forward. As he steps inside, lights on the ceiling come on, one at a time, making us both jump. And I think I kind of remember it. Remember the footprint-worn floors. The circle lights on the ceiling. The doors. But maybe I'm remembering something else. A dream. A nightmare.

I don't remember the flying dots, though. They buzz around, sounding like electricity.

I step in after Willow and he shimmies round me, picking a rock up from the floor and jamming it right into the door, keeping it open.

I look at him. He don't look excited no more. He looks afraid. But he looks at me like he knows who I am.

He don't.

I take his hand in mine. His fingers feel cold.

I lead the way. I walk slowly through the clouds of black dots, eyes down, passing clean door after clean door.

'Aren't you going to try these?' he whispers behind me.

No.

I keep walking. Until I get to the one where all the footprints stop. Where the key to the door is just sitting on the floor, waiting for me to come on back.

Where the smell is coming from.

Willow chokes as we stand Outside. 'What *is* that?' he says again.

And my head is all full of noise. My blood is fizzing with a thousand things. My ears are drumming gunshots. And, with every bang, a new picture comes shooting into my head. Of Cow. Of Bee. Of Queenie. Of them all smiling up at me, playing with me and telling me that everything is going to be OK.

And then there's that door. That door.

What's behind the door, Ele?

I screw my eyes up and ram my hands into them.

No. I got to be brave. It hurts more than anything He ever did to me. More than broken jaws and bloody knuckles. But I got through that. I did. And I can get through this.

Once upon a time, there was a girl who lived in a Tower, and she was alone.

My shaking fingers claw hold of Willow. He's looking at me like he's struggling to see through the smell, and I know. I feel it, too, burning my eyes, pushing into my nose and lips.

I pull his head forward and into his ear I whisper, 'Please don't hate me.'

I pull away before I can see the confused look on his face. Before he can ask me why. Why would he hate me? Why am I being so weird? What could I have possibly done that's so bad?

I bend down and I pick up the key, red streaks dried up on it now. I turn and I give it to him.

'What? Are they in here?' he says, and I see it in his face. Fear. The whites of his eyes are haunted with sudden thoughts.

I can't lie no more.

How to set things right – number three: Tell the truth.

I shake my head. I shake it until Willow has to put his hands on my shoulders and stop me, but still – *still* – I don't stop looking at him. 'Cause I know it'll be the last time he looks at me like that. I ball up his sweater in my fist, trying to catch my thoughts.

Are they in there, Ele? Are they?

My breath builds and builds, and I wonder if I'm gonna be sick.

All the time, he looks at me.

'No.' It comes out of me like a moan, like someone is twisting up my stomach from the inside. I double over. 'No, no, no, no, no.'

And it hurts. It hurts and it hurts. All this bad is coming up out of me – up and up – ripping at my throat and my head. I want to swallow it back down, but it needs to come out.

It's time. It hurts, but it's time.

I steady myself on his shoulder, and his hand wraps round mine.

'What's wrong?'

I spit the last of it from my head. Stand up. Look at his wide eyes.

And I tell him the truth.

'The Others ain't in there.' My voice sounds like poison. 'And they never was.'

I step back, pulling him with me, leading him and the key towards the door.

'I made them up.'

I bring his hand and the key down on to the keypad and the door bursts open.

FIFTY-TWO

It started as a game.

We was so small when He locked us in there. Zeb and me. At first, we thought He'd be letting us out in no time. It weren't the first time He'd locked us away. In cupboards and in rooms.

He'd locked us in with her then, though. Our mother. And when she was there things never seemed so bad. We might have been squished together in dark, dusty places, but she lit them up with stories and songs. We'd play games and have so much fun we'd sometimes wish He'd never open the door again.

But then we was in the Tower. And she weren't there that time.

We were alone.

Every day, Zeb thought up ways for us to escape. Banging on the door. Trying to reach the sun bars. Trying to sneak past when He came in.

We was only little then. No one heard us banging on the door, and we couldn't reach the sun bars. When we tried to sneak past Him, He'd beat us so bad that we was tasting blood for weeks. He caught us. Every time.

He was being all nice to me sometimes, too, telling me pretty things about how this was my home now. A home He went and built just for me and din I like it?

Zeb got more and more angry and weren't as fun as he used to be. He made me run all the time. He told me scary stories of what He was going to do to us. Zeb kept reminding me that He'd taken us and trapped us Inside.

And, after a while, I kept thinking, weren't it better to think of it His way? Weren't it better to live in a story where I was in my very own home, built just for me? So, just like our mother used to do, I filled our Tower with stories.

Even when He was less nice and started to make me do things I din like, it became easier and easier to escape from all that. The more I invented my stories, the more real they became. And so, when we got too big for our clothes and He took them away, that was OK, 'cause there never was no clothes to begin with, right? And, when He did the bad things, that was OK, 'cause it wasn't for long, and the stories were right there again after.

But Zeb couldn't live in the story like I could. He stayed in the real and started dying inside himself, bit by bit. He would just stay in his corner, staring into nothing, sadness eating him up.

And that's when the Others appeared, jumping right out of the books and becoming as real as if they were always there. They were my friends. They looked like Goblins and were mighty crafty like the ones in the books, but they were also sweet as sweet could be. Cow with his simple eyes. Bee with her love of touching. And Queenie, who always got the story going.

I wanted Zeb to play, too. But he din.

I don't remember when it stopped being a game and started being real. The two started muddling together in my head, and I saw everything as if it *was* real.

When Zeb died, things din seem right. I started to see things how he'd seen them. I started to see the walls again.

So I began trying to pick through my lies. Separate the truths from the reals. Was I Inside, or was Inside all there was? Sometimes I was mighty sure that there *was* an Outside, with trees and rivers and all. But then there was that other side of me that din want to think of that – not unless I really had to. 'Cause if there *was* an Outside, then I'd been Inside all that time. And I'd kept Zeb away from that Outside.

Now that door is open and I know the real truth. And so does Willow.

FIFTY-THREE

I never thought a smell could be as powerful as a Giant.

This one is. It grips at our throats, pushing itself into our mouths, our eyes, everywhere. It stuffs itself inside of us and empties us out. We become it. And it's so bad. So, so bad.

We don't need to see Inside. Instead, we run back down the long room, retching and heaving. The buzzing black dots whip at our faces. And when we get out, the Outside air feels like breathing again.

We both fall to the ground. I dig my fingers into the tiny stones. My hands are shaking.

'Ele!' Willow chokes out. 'Ele!'

He ain't really looking for me, though. He's looking all around him, eyes white. He stumbles around, looking bad.

All their faces are in my eyes. Bee. Cow. Queenie.

I'm sick again.

'What's in there?' he says, dragging himself away from the door.

I spit. 'Him.' I turn to sit on my hands to stop them shaking. 'It's Him.'

'Oh, Jesus,' Willow says, hands all over his face. 'Oh, shit.' Then he looks at me. He looks at me hard. And I can't tear my eyes away, even though I don't want to see that look. I can't lie no more, though. Not to myself. Not to no one.

'Did you . . .' He wipes his hand over his face. 'Did you know about this?'

I keep my eyes on him. I keep them there.

'Yes.' My voice is still clogged up with all the bad.

Willow stares at me, shaking his head. 'Fuck.'

'Yes,' I say again, and my voice is all broken.

He leans over, his head in his hands. 'Oh, shit. Oh, shit. Oh, shit. I thought –' he says, voice all muffled. 'I didn't think, Ele. I –'

He sounds like a little 'un.

I push myself to my feet, my head still clouded up.

Willow stumbles up, too, folding his arms round himself. I think he's looking at me until I see his eyes are all out of focus. I turn round and spot what he's really looking at: a figure marching up the hill towards us, arms swaying. My belly kicks.

Ezra-Dad.

Willow don't even pause for a second. Soon as he knows it's him, he lets out a sigh and runs shakily towards him, looking all small compared to Ezra-Dad, even though he's higher up the hill. As he gets closer, the moon lights up the concern on Ezra-Dad's face.

'What –' Ezra-Dad starts.

But his words are taken as Willow throws himself into Ezra-Dad's arms, wrapping his own arms round him, clutching on. Ezra-Dad halts, surprise only stopping him for a second from squeezing Willow back. And then he does. He hugs him, and he hugs him hard.

I watch them together. A wind blows up cold.

Willow is speaking really fast, but his words get less and less like shaky cries and more like words as they pull apart and walk towards me. And, as they do, both of their stares find me.

I step away.

Willow stops when he reaches me, but Ezra-Dad keeps on marching towards the Tower, only his hand on Willow's shoulder stopping him from going all the way. He swings back, free hand scratching through his beard, his face all shadow.

'In there?' he says. 'In that one?'

'Aye,' Willow says, wiping his nose on his sleeve.

Ezra-Dad nods, looking at me. 'Ye OK?'

I nod back.

'OK,' he says, and I can almost see the thoughts dashing around his eyes. 'OK.'

I pull my hands up into the sleeves of my coat, shivering. I can see an awful lot from this hill. The mountains. Lights from the windows of houses. All these places where people are living without knowing all of this is even going on.

Ezra-Dad looks at me again, and I know he's gone and come to a decision.

'Give me yer phone, Will.'

Willow looks up at him, before darting a look at me. 'Why?' he says.

'We need tae call the police.'

'But, Dad,' Willow says, shifting from foot to foot. 'They'll . . . I mean, what will they do to Ele?'

Ezra-Dad sighs, putting his spare hand on my shoulder, linking himself to Willow and me. He looks at me sadly. And I know. I know people need to know now.

How to be an Outside Person – number five: Tell the truth.

'She'll be fine.'

And I nod. *It's OK.*

'No,' Willow says, ducking from under Ezra-Dad's hand. 'Dad, they'll take her away. They'll think that she . . . she *did* this.'

Ezra-Dad looks at me out of the corner of his eye. And I know that he already knows.

I did.

'They willnae think that,' he says.

But Willow is shaking his head, hands running through his hair. 'We can . . . We'll . . . we'll hide it somehow.'

'Will –' Ezra-Dad starts.

'No, Dad!' Willow shouts over him, all his fear tumbling over anger. 'I . . . I promised that I'd look after her. I promised.'

Ezra-Dad squeezes his shoulder and Willow looks at him. And, even though they look mighty different, I reckon they're almost the same now, in the dark.

'And ye've done a damn fine job, lad. Better than ah –' He swallows and looks up at the stars like he's wishing on them.

'Ah shouldnae have waited so long tae do it. Soon as ah met ye, ah knew something was up.' He squeezes my shoulder tighter, and looks back to Willow. 'We need tae call the police now, Will. OK?'

Willow looks at me. I nod.

Slowly, Willow takes his phone out of his pocket and hands it to him. Ezra-Dad lets go of my arm to make the call.

And, as soon as his hand leaves my shoulder, I run.

FIFTY-FOUR

My legs are empty. I stumble down the hill, my heartbeat filling my ears. I trip over something sticking up out of the ground and fall sideways, turning the world purple.

I drag myself up. There are rocks in my arms.

'Ele!'

Willow. Running after me, wheezing already.

'Stay back!' I shout, but it sounds more like a whisper. I try running again, but my legs bottom out from under me and I fall again, this time on to my knees.

The pain feels like cold in my bones.

'Ele!'

Again, I stumble up. Again, I fall – but this time he's there to catch me. He falls, too, so we're both down on the ground.

'Leave –' I gasp. 'Leave me alone!'

'Nae,' he says. 'Let me help.'

I shake my head, trying to fight him off, but I don't have nothing left. I don't.

'Let me help,' he says again, pulling my head up and looking into my eyes.

I see myself reflected in them. And it's stupid, but I don't look no different.

I thought I would.

I hold his face. It feels warm in my icy fingers.

'No,' I say, and my voice don't sound like mine. It sounds like it's bleeding. 'I lied about it all. About the Others. About Him.'

Still he looks at me. Still he holds me. 'They weren't lies, Ele. They were . . .' He pulls me closer to him. He's shaking. 'What the hell happened there?'

I shake my head into his sweater. 'Everything. Nothing.'

'Did –' He swallows. 'I can't believe I'm asking this.' He strokes the hair out of my face. 'Did He . . . keep you? There?'

He ain't looking me in the eye.

'Yes.'

'For how long?' His voice has gone all high. Still he strokes my hair. His hand feels heavy.

'Long,' I say.

He nods, his lips pressed tight. 'And the Others you told me about?'

I squeeze my eyes shut. *I'm sorry, Bee. I'm sorry.*

'I made them up.'

'Good,' he says, and my eyes fly open. 'I'm pleased no one else had to go through that shit.'

He looks at me now, eyes full of sad.

'Just . . . Ele. Will you forgive me?'

I lean back. 'Forgive you?'

He licks his lips. 'I didn't know, you know? I thought . . . Well, I didn't think. And all this time you were carrying all this and then I brought you back here.' He shakes his head. 'I was excited to come here tonight. *Excited*.'

Everything in me is numb and cold. I can hear Ezra-Dad talking on the phone. Words like 'body' and 'dead' float over to where we are – not even that far away – but they don't mean nothing now.

'How did . . .?' Willow says.

I wrap the tassels of his jumper round my fingers. 'I . . . I must have shot him,' I say. 'He had his gun out, and he was gonna kill me like he killed Zeb, so . . .'

'Shit,' Willow says. He doesn't let go of me. 'Zeb? The one you told me about before? Back in the shed?'

I nod.

'He was in there, too?'

Eyes all wide. Blood circling the drain.

I nod again, and I need to remember that Willow don't know all this. He don't know the story or the truth and it's OK to be asking questions.

'It was my fault,' I whisper, feeling the pain twang in my belly again.

He shakes his head, holding my arms. 'Ele, none of this is your fault. OK?'

Yes, it is.

'Ele, look at me.'

I open my eyes.

'It's not your fault.'

I close them again. He grabs me harder, pulling me up all clumsy to my feet.

'I won't let anything bad happen to you,' he says.

I can hear them now. Sirens, like the ones on TV. Sounding all strange in the dark, like dying animals.

'It can't be like this,' he groans.

I turn to him, and he's looking all around us like he's hoping to find the answers out in the dark.

'The Others – you're *sure* they're not real?'

His words hurt my ears. I nod.

'What about . . . ' he says. 'What about Jack?'

I freeze. 'Jack?'

'Your friend, right? Well, what about him?'

I choke. 'Just knocks on walls,' I say, but goddamn it. *Goddamn it, Jack*. I'd forgotten Jack. Is Jack lies or truth?

'OK,' Willow says, grabbing my arms, a spark of something back in his eyes. 'OK. Tell me everything. Start from the beginning.'

The beginning.

'I don't know,' I say. 'It was after Zeb went. I was feeling mighty lonely and . . . and his knocks were there.'

'What do you mean, knocks?' Willow says, starting to walk me back up the hill. Ezra-Dad is sitting on the floor, head in his hands. We stride past him.

'On the walls,' I say, trying to look behind me, trying to see whether Ezra-Dad is hating me. 'On my wall.'

Willow pushes me into the smell.

'Wait,' I say, but he don't.

'Which wall?'

We cough as we enter the building again. My legs are fighting him. They dig in their heels.

Don't make me go back in.

'The . . . right side.'

'And this –' he coughs – 'this was after Zeb got killed?'

I nod, my eyes streaming.

'And how exactly did he die?'

Don't make me say it.

I moan. 'He shot him.'

'Are you sure?' Willow says, looking back over his shoulder through squinted eyes. 'Are you sure he was dead when He left?'

'Yes!' I shout, trying to get out of his grip. 'He was shot in the head! He lifted His gun up and hit him right over the head with it. There was . . . there was blood.'

We're at the Tower entrance again. The door is ajar and I know what's on the other side. I know it. But Willow don't make me go through. He pulls me to the door next to it – the one on the right. He covers his face with his arm and bends down to pick up the key we dropped. The key all smudged up with His blood.

When he stands up, his face is flashing with blue lights. 'Ele, that's not what being shot means.'

I feel myself getting angry at being called wrong – even under what he's saying. But then Willow lifts the key up to the door next to my Tower. The light above it goes green. And it's a different kind of smell in here. Bad, but not dead.

Willow pushes the door and opens up a room full of darkness. I grip the wall, recognizing everything in there as the Inside I know. I *knew*.

It's so small.

But I understand what Willow is saying. This ain't my Tower. This is another room, one that lived all this time on the other side of my wall.

This is Jack's room.

I push the door further, blue lights now flashing around the Inside. The tap. The drain in the middle. The food bowl – empty. But there's something else. A shape in the corner. A bag of bones and tangled hair.

I choke, gripping the door. 'Zeb?'

My brother. Curled up in the corner, fists all bloody from knocking.

He's alive.

FIFTY-FIVE

I'm tangled up in Zeb on the floor of the room. There are lights, but I can't see them. There's noise, but I can't hear it. I'm making a noise. I can feel it in my chest, humming like I've swallowed all the black dots flying around. I can't hear it, though. The Others have got their hands on my ears again.

His body is all bones. There are rough patches of skin all over him, like he's been grating himself over the walls and the floor. He's breathing like it takes all of him to do it. His whole ribs throw themselves wide with each breath, and his dry, broken lips look like they are screaming, too.

He clutches me back. I don't know if he knows it's me. He don't look at me long enough to see.

They come in. They try to take me away from him, but I don't let go. They ask me questions, but I can't hear them over all this noise of nothing.

Then things start breaking through, one at a time. The yellow lights they're shining on us. A question.

'What is your name?'

I'm being ripped up. I'm being screwed and wound round. 'He's me!' I shout. 'He's me!'

He does look like me. A me before Willow. But worse. So much worse.

I can hear Willow. He's telling them who we are. He's sorting the lies from the truths. The Inside from the Outside.

He's not me. He's Zeb.

He's *alive*.

Each moment is being measured out by flashes of light. The noise of people talking, cussing. We're watched with sad eyes.

'Ele,' one of them is saying, holding my elbow. 'Ele, can you let us look at Zeb?'

I don't want to let go. I wind myself further up in his hair, and he grips at me.

I don't want to let him go. I just found him again.

'Ele, it's time for Zeb to get out now.'

And it is. It was all those years ago, when we first started trying.

It's my fault.

I let go of him, but keep his arm in my hand. It fits easily, like I'm holding a finger.

The people are wearing green coats. Zeb is doing his best to shout and hide away, but he don't have no voice or nothing left to do that with.

'It's OK,' I whisper to him in Other. In our language. 'It's OK.'

They look him over. Shine lights in his eyes. Listen to his chest through a wire. Wrap blankets over him. They lay him down on a board and thread needles into his arms, put a see-through bucket over his face and cover his eyes up, even though it's still night. They try to put a blanket over me, too. They try to take me out and away, but I won't leave him. He leaves that place with me, holding my hand. Him lying down and being carried by the people in green coats. Me walking next to him.

We pass my Tower – what used to be *our* Tower – but I don't look Inside, even though the door is open and the people are inside there, too. I only see the shape on the floor out of the corner of my eye. I hope Zeb can't smell Him through his mask. He can't hurt us no more.

'It's OK,' I say. Again and again and again.

They load us up into a big, bright hunk of junk full of laptops and wires and things I want to touch. But I don't let go of Zeb's hand. Or his eyes. The only time I look up is as they are closing the doors, and I see Ezra-Dad arguing with a man in black who is holding a black box to his ear that's also talking to him. And I see Willow looking back at me.

He smiles.

I hope I smile back.

PART FOUR

OUTSIDE OUTSIDE

FIFTY-SIX

'Slow down!' I call out to Willow, who's marching ahead.

'Nae. Keep up!'

I cuss under my breath and scurry along to join him.

We've been walking for ages, and we were driving for ages before that. Willow ain't told me where we're going. He just asked me to pack some stuff into the picnic basket and put on my sun cream.

It's damn hot.

There ain't no people here. We're up high, away from our house and the town with the hospitals and the reporters and the police. The ground is spongy and brown. I want to stop and touch it, but Willow won't let me.

'Slow down!' I call again.

He just turns and flashes me a smile.

We're not supposed to be outside. Doctor Kelly told me that my skin ain't used to the sun yet, so I got to stay inside in the day. But Willow says that ain't nothing that can't be solved by sun cream and an umbrella.

I feel stupid carrying around an umbrella when it ain't raining.

Doctor Kelly likes making up rules almost as much as I do, but she's all right, really. She's mighty good at getting to the truth of the matter, and she lets me know all of the truths – the good and the bad. Ezra-Dad ain't always pleased with the stuff she tells me, but I tell him that it's better to know than not.

Truths are like people, see. They don't like being shut up tight. They shrivel slowly, and then they rot with lies, creating something mighty ugly. Something so bad you'll need to throw out all your clothes, 'cause you'll still smell it on you days – *weeks* – after. Even after a thousand washes.

And when those truths get out in the open you might think they're gonna smell up the whole world. Rub their backs on the clouds and turn them grey. Wilt the bloom out of the moon. But they don't. They get rubbed clean by people. Nice people.

They come back to life. They grow up like trees into something new.

It turns out that the job of the police is to find out the truths. And, after we'd had the first few of our chats up in her office, Doctor Kelly said that I could find them out, too.

How to be an Outside Person – number twenty-one: Find out the real truth.

I found out a lot.

His name was Brian Colt. He'd come over here from a place called the United States of America a long time ago. He had done some bad things over there that had 'slipped through the net'. He'd brought a lady with him – my mother. He wasn't very nice to her, but she stayed with Him even though her door was open.

They had twins – Zeb and me. Twins means we've shared the same space all of our lives. No one knew about us. Not one person. We din exist on the Outside.

They din realize she was dead neither, 'til they found her body buried behind His house.

I guess she never did find her brave.

Her name was Janet. They showed me a picture of her. With that yellow hair and those red lips smiling. Just like I remembered her in my dreams.

Doctor Kelly asked me if I was mad at her for not doing something. For not taking Zeb and me and running away from Him, back when we still could have. But, when I think about it, I don't reckon I do feel mad, 'cause she did get us out in her own way, din she? She read us those stories and she taught us how to read and how to speak. She taught us how to be brave, even though she couldn't be.

I keep her picture in a frame next to my bed.

They guess that He killed her, and that's when things got worse for Zeb and me. He had the stables specially built. There were six rooms in all. *Six.* I asked Doctor Kelly why there were six rooms when he'd only used two, and she told me that was a very good question.

I reckon I'll be a police officer one day.

He controlled the rooms with electricity. It was clever, they said, for a man who dealt in scraps. Water was on tap, as was the cleaning solution that rained down from the ceiling. But the rest – the lights, the food, the doors – He controlled.

They found out what He did to me when He visited, too. I told Doctor Kelly on my second visit to her office. She asked me if it was OK for her to tell anyone else, but I said that I ain't telling no more lies. It made Ezra-Dad crumble at the middle when he heard, like a building falling down.

They don't know why He kept Zeb alive. They just have theories. Theories about selling him on to other people. But theories ain't truth – they're just scary stories.

They found out about the day I escaped, too. I told Doctor Kelly about it as best I could, but it was mighty hard not to lie to her. In the end, she asked me to tell her the lying version *and* the version I thought to be truth. That was easier. She's helping me to work it all out. To separate things into lists of stories and truths.

Of course, the Others din take the gun off Him. It was me. But I don't remember what I did. All I remember is the darkness, like their hands are still over my eyes and my ears. They're still protecting me.

All we know of the truth is that He was hit on the head a lot, knocking him out cold for enough time for me to escape. Not enough to kill Him, mind. And it's good to know – even after everything He did – that I weren't the one who killed Him.

When I escaped, the door slammed shut. The key dropped to the floor Outside. And He was trapped in that Tower, in the dark. When He woke up, He ate all the feed left in the bowl. And then nothing. Not for days and days. There weren't no feed rattling down the pipes, and no light coming on day and night.

And it was the same for Zeb. Nothing.

When they found Him, He had a hole in His head – right between the eyes. Turns out that guns can explode a head, just like they can explode a wall. They said He did it to Himself. It's funny, ain't it? We always thought Him bigger and stronger than us. But He weren't that strong, after all.

Zeb was as strong as ten Giants. I guess he was used to not eating much. It weren't the first time he'd lived without food and light for a while, if his Tower was anything like mine. So he ate only what he needed to from the feed left inside the bowl. Filled the rest of himself up with drink. Just like I would've done.

They said he wouldn't have lasted much longer if we hadn't gone back, though. I cling to that truth and try to forget the feeling inside me that I should've gone back sooner. That I should've known. That I left him in the dark while I ate and stayed with a family and became almost real. Sometimes I get awful sad about all of that, but Doctor Kelly helps. So do Willow and Ezra-Dad.

Zeb ain't as concerned with the facts as me. He ain't concerned about much, truth be told. I see him as much as I can. He's in a special place called a hospital, but I make sure they keep the door open for him. He has a bed, though his is on wheels and not as comfy as mine. He has a wardrobe with clothes in it, too, and lots of people have been sending him cards and toys and stuff, which I show him when I go. We even got him a phone when I got mine so I can talk to him, even when we ain't together. He don't know how to use it yet, but I send him messages, anyway.

GET BETTER, ZEB.

Mainly he just stares around when I'm there, not really looking. Never talking. But he does like me speaking in Other. When I do it, he clutches at me like he knows who I am.

The doctors there do the same tests on me as they do on him. Tests on my eyes, my ears, my legs. Tests where I need to talk a lot. Tell more truths. Some of them are helpful. Some of them ain't.

I like the words they use on me, though. 'Remarkable'. 'Strong'. 'Unique'. They can't believe a girl who has been Inside so long can be as brilliant as me, and it feels good to be liked by all these people. Everyone wants to talk to me – all these people in white coats and black coats and red coats. And all the Outside People. The TV wants to talk to me. And Willow says there are people all over the internet talking about me, too. I don't need to talk to them, though. I don't even care what no one thinks of me but Willow and Ezra-Dad, which Doctor Kelly says is a real good thing.

They don't use those magic words on Zeb. His words are 'damaged', 'trauma' and 'malnourished'. But Zeb lived in the truth of it all for so long. He soaked it up for the both of us, while I lived all dry in my lies. My brother. And he taught me to run every day, so I'd be fit to do it when the time came. He taught me to seek out the truth when I was ready to hear it. He saved me.

When he's better, he can come stay with me in my new home with Ezra-Dad and Willow. We can redecorate Willow's old room together and make it ours. He can listen to me as I learn the violin. Willow is teaching me, and I reckon I'm getting good. I even got my own one, all shiny wood. I can show Zeb all the friends Ezra-Dad and I are planting for Maple – flowers of all different sorts. We're even gonna plant an Ash soon, to grow up with Maple.

And maybe Zeb can have a journal, too. A blank book to write his own story in, just like I'm doing. A book of truth.

And he can come on secret walks with Willow and me.

'OK, we're here!' Willow calls.

I've been buried in my own head for a while. When I finally lift it up and look around, I ain't so sure that I ain't still in there, 'cause it looks just like that Outside Inside my Head. I'm standing on a hill, the toes of my brand-new trainers buried in tiny spikes of green grass. When I look down the hill, I see water running fast – blue and white in places, and sounding like tiny things talking. And there's a big rock next to it, where Willow is sitting himself down, taking out the food I packed and laying it all out for us to eat.

I see it and I don't see it.

I let my umbrella fall and see that the sun is being broken into tiny pieces by leaves. Green . . . and *real*. Growing on trees so tall they scoop up clouds as they float through the sky. And I can hear whistling from the branches, and smell the flowers, and taste the green in my mouth.

'I thought you'd like it,' Willow says, beaming at me.

He wants me to go over to him. Wants me to sit next to him on the rock. To take off my shoes, dip my feet in the water and listen to the wind in the trees. And I want to do all those things, too. And I will. In a moment.

For now, I close my eyes. I take a deep breath. And I send out my knocks to Zeb in that hospital.

Zeb, I knock. *We've found it. The Proof of the Outside.*

ACKNOWLEDGEMENTS

This book was made by hundreds of brilliant people over twelve years (and three 'practice' stories). To everyone who told me what to do, and that I could – thank you. I'm sorry I can't list you all here.

My fantastic family have been there every step of the way. Thanks for staying up until two in the morning to read my drafts, Mum. And Dad – thanks for queueing with me at midnight for the next Harry Potter book. Grandma and Grandad – you're only allowed to buy *two* copies. Put this one down and leave the poor bookseller alone.

Kathryn Davies, Anna Raby and Harriet Venn – you are the very best friends a weird girl could have. Harriet – the plan worked!

My wonderful agent, Sallyanne Sweeney, who sent me a life-changing email forty-four minutes after receiving *Outside*. Your belief in my writing is phenomenal – thank you.

Thanks also to my fabulous editor Carmen McCullough for championing this book and making it shine. And Kimberley Davis, Wendy Shakespeare, Shreeta Shah and the whole PRH Children's team – you are all amazing.

Acknowledgements

A big shout out to the many writing groups I've been a part of over the years, with special thanks to the writers and tutors at Arvon Totleigh Barton 2014, and the Advanced Writing Workshop 2016 with tutor Catherine Smith.

Ellie Brough and Pippa Lewis – you are my favourite people to write with. Ellie – thank you for sending me screenshots of your favourite pages and forwarding them to your mum to check the Scottish. Pippa – thank you for explaining what this book is *really* about. You were right, as always.

My original proofreaders: the Venn sisters, Anna Lewis, Ryan Annis and Helen Leale-Green.

Thanks also to the Annis family, for allowing me space in their summerhouse to write this. Ryan, Jacquie and Chris – your support over the last few years has been tremendous, thank you.

I've been extremely lucky to work with some of the best people on the planet, who gave me everything from unwavering belief to writing retreat Christmas bonuses. The teams at Blaby Library Group, Completely Novel, Creative Future, the NSPCC and Jericho Writers – you rule.

And finally thank *you* for reading all the way to the very end of this book. You might be my most favourite person of all.

ABOUT THE AUTHOR

Sarah Ann Juckes is a Content Creator for Jericho Writers and lives in East Sussex, UK. *Outside* was shortlisted for Mslexia's Children's Novel competition and longlisted for the Bath Novel Award. She volunteers for the NSPCC's 'Speak Out and Stay Safe' programme, and is on the board of Creative Future, working with under-represented writers.

www.sarahannjuckes.com
@sarahannjuckes